ELIZABETH WALCOTT-HACKSHAW

MRS. B

A NOVEL

D1354487

PEEPAL TREE

First published in Great Britain in 2014
Peepal Tree Press Ltd
17 King's Avenue
Leeds LS6 1QS
England

ISBN13: 9781845232313

The poem quoted on page 34 is "Love after Love"
by Derek Walcott from *Sea Grapes* (1976)

Supported using public funding by
ARTS COUNCIL
ENGLAND

# CONTENTS

*For my father, for his kindness*

# PART ONE

# CHAPTER ONE
## ARRIVALS – TRINIDAD JUNE 2009

On the day that Ruthie returned home, six people were killed in the beautiful Valencia Valley. A popular pigtail vendor was amongst the six. According to police reports, Mr. Phillip Michael Beharry, 54, was shot in front of his barbecue pit at 6 pm on the evening of June 19th, Labour Day. It was alleged that the shooting was an act of revenge since Mr. Beharry had apparently been involved in an altercation with a young man the previous evening at "The Den", a bar opposite Beharry's pigtail outlet. The young man allegedly returned the following evening and shot Beharry three times in the head and once in the stomach. On arrival at the Southern Presbyterian Community Hospital, Mr. Phillip Michael Beharry, popular barbecued pigtail owner, was pronounced dead.

★

Charles had read the article on Beharry earlier that morning. The seven o'clock radio news was giving the story a longer life than most murders on the island, but it had nothing to do with Beharry himself; Beharry was murder number 360, doubling the murder toll on the same date from the previous year. 360 murdered in six months; this was an island record. Beharry's biography even took up more time than the slight mention given to Uriah Buzz Butler and his famous protest march on June 19th 1937. Charles's father had been a great fan of Butler and had spoken to his young son of Butler's courage. Charles remembered little of what his father had said to him but he'd liked the name "Buzz Butler".

Charles was still trying to get the football score. He had missed the sports report, and now it was only the weather forecast for the following day. He almost knew it by heart: "…waves up to two metres in open water, one point five in sheltered areas…" The only numbers that mattered was the result of the USA – Brazil match at the Confederations Cup in South Africa, on which he'd had a bet with his good buddy, Chow. Charles was about to complain to his wife that he was tired of the toll number on the front page of every newspaper every morning, as though there was nothing else happening in the damn country, or around the world, but he said nothing and consoled himself with the idea of finding the score on the FIFA website later that evening, or maybe sneaking a call to Chow at the airport. He didn't dare to take his eyes off the road for even a second (the carnage on the roads competed with the murder toll) but he managed to glance across at his wife at a red traffic light. She looked far away, her thoughts no doubt with their daughter who was flying in that evening.

"We'll be late," she said, breaking away from the trance.

"We have time; the flight doesn't get in until eight."

"I was thinking about her name. She's always hated her name. 'Why did you call me Ruth? It's such an ugly name.' Remember she used to say that all the time in primary school, in high school as well. I can't remember why we chose Ruth instead of something prettier, like Nicole or even Nina. Marie Claire Nicole Butcher. But then we still had to deal with your hatchet of a name. Isn't that right, Mr. Butcher?" Mrs. B tried to force a smile but Charles knew she wasn't joking. It was why she was known as Mrs. B and never Mrs. Butcher, and she was the one who'd insisted on Ruth, a name she had found in a novel she was reading at the time. Charles knew better than to say any of this, not now, not tonight, and luckily she didn't demand an answer or talk again until they reached the airport car park at 7:30 pm.

"Remember not to say anything about Boston," she said after closing the car door in the parking lot.

"What would I say, Elena?"

She didn't reply, just kept walking a step or two ahead of her husband, quick short steps, high heels click click on the paved ground, her black dress swishing slightly, enhancing her neat figure and small waist. Charles wanted to tell her that she looked lovely, that she should relax, that everything would be okay with Ruthie. April was April. This was June; it was over now; she was

10

coming home, she was better. But he just followed his wife mutely, trying to tuck his shirt into khaki trousers that were too tight.

The night before they had dinner with friends who toasted Ruthie's return. No one mentioned what had happened during the spring break, though they all knew at least part of the story – the part about the nervous breakdown. They congratulated Mrs. B on having such a brilliant daughter, graduating summa cum laude no less. They reminded Mrs. B of the fabulous party she'd had for Ruthie after the Open Scholarship award was announced. On that evening everything shone, except Ruthie herself, who never wanted the attention. Mrs. B had invited fifty guests to the party on the verandah of their sprawling five-acre home in the valley: waiters, waitresses, champagne, samosas, smoked salmon, dim sum, shrimp, sushi. The front lawn was lit with tall bamboo torches; heliconias, tall red gingers and blood-red anthuriums filled huge clay pots on the verandah. Everything seemed perfect and even the two mosaic dolphins at the bottom of the pool seemed to smile with pride. Mrs. B, elegant and gracious, greeted each guest warmly, as though they were the most important person to enter her home. This was four years ago. So much had happened since then.

Ruthie had a few friends there. She didn't surround herself with a troupe like her mother, didn't like too many people around her. Though she was not a head-turner like her mother, Ruthie's face could pull you in the more you looked, but she seldom smiled and usually had a serious look, as though she was resisting her prettiness. When people complimented her light brown eyes that seemed to sparkle against her olive skin, she barely acknowledged the compliment. Ruthie was not impolite, always said "Uncle this" or "Auntie that", but she was not what her Martinican aunts would call *souriante*. Ruthie just looked as though she didn't see the point of the perpetual grin that most of her mother's friends always wore, like their lipstick. Ruthie did well in school, she had a good memory, one that could help her pass exams, help her cram – that was her true talent – so she won the end of term prizes, moved up easily from one standard to the other, crossed from one's Dean's list to another, but always without passion or pride. She knew she was bright but she certainly wasn't the genius her mother claimed she was; all the light shining on her made Ruthie want to disappear. Mainly she felt like a fraud.

★

On that Labour Day evening, Ruthie was barely showing, but her face betrayed the anxiety she was trying to hide. From the plane, across the tarmac, into the cold building, feeling nauseous, she made her way through the long immigration lines (no stopping at duty free for gifts); picked up her baggage; lined up (nothing to declare) to emerge from the no man's land between Custom's officer and country, between what she left behind and what she brought home.

She walked out from the stale, air-conditioned, suitcase-smelling room into the thick hot island air to face the exhaust fumes of idling car engines. No more the broad Bostonian "paark the caar in Haarvard yaard", but Trinidadian sing-song, up and down intonations; a "Taxi Miss" here, a "Taxi Miss" there, a crowd bunched together looking wary and hopeful, as each new traveller emerged from those magic doors, to face whatever it meant to be home.

Ruthie later claimed she had no idea that she had smuggled a baby (smuggled was the word she used) through the Customs, but Mrs. B couldn't believe that her daughter didn't know. She could not bring herself to say her daughter was a liar, but was unable to stop herself thinking that more trouble had arrived with her daughter, and that soon all her friends would know. Later, Mrs. B confided *in confidence* to her dear friends Jackie and Kathy, who passed on the news until everyone knew, but pretended that they didn't. When Ruthie really started to show, no one was surprised, although they all pretended that they were.

★

Mrs. B nudged her way to the front of the crowd at the exit doors. She wanted to see what condition Ruthie was in. Charles had not accompanied her to Boston two months before; his excuse was the business. Charles' cowardice no longer surprised her; she'd had to deal with many stressful, sad, even tragic incidents throughout their marriage without him, although this time it did seem strange since he seldom hid behind the excuse of business when it involved Ruthie.

April would go down as one of the worst months in Mrs. B's life, cruel in every way. Boston was still very cold and Ruthie's attitude towards her even colder. Ruthie was distant, like a stranger; she barely spoke to anyone in the psychiatric clinic. The day Mrs. B arrived in Boston she visited Ruthie's roommate, Alice, who gave her the entire story. Alice had found Ruthie on the floor of their bathroom at four o'clock in the afternoon. Alice, short, stocky, effusive, Jewish, insisted on describing the unnatural position of Ruthie's body which had made her think that Ruthie was dead. The vomit had streaks of blood in it, a thin watery string flowed out of Ruthie's mouth, and the floor was slimy, the empty bottles of pills right there. She had puked in Ruthie's vomit before she called the concierge, who called the security guard for the building. Mrs. B did not want any more details, but Alice seemed to need the repetition, for she described this scene several times during Mrs. B's stay in Boston.

Mrs. B tried hard to erase the image of her daughter on the bathroom floor, with the horrible mess everywhere and felt irritated, embarrassed and ashamed that it was *her* daughter who had collapsed in front of everyone. She felt even more ashamed for feeling ashamed. Still, she was grateful to this chatty friend who had saved her daughter from God knows what. "Thank you, Alice," Mrs. B said, and had Alice been Caribbean and not American, Mrs. B would have hugged her there and then, but instead she took Alice's hand and held it in her own.

*

As she left the safety of the airport, Ruthie suddenly wanted to vomit. Her stomach was churning around a mixture of guilt, anger and embarrassment. Then it hit her worse than anything she had been through in recent months – and God knows she had been through a lot – it hit her like a slap from an old boyfriend, or a fall on hard ice: she still had feelings for the Professor, still felt something for *le loup* – the code name used by her dear friend Eddy.

Eddy was one of the few American friends she had made and cared about during her time in Boston; from the first time they spoke in an English Literature class, she trusted him instinctively – which surprised her because trust did not come to her naturally. When she found out that Eddy was gay she loved him even more; there would be no pressure. Eddy had helped her pack up in the last few days, getting her ready to leave Boston, getting her ready to leave *le loup* behind. Now, just when Ruthie thought she had finally escaped, the old feelings re-emerged, threatening to spoil the composure she had managed for her return home.

But now, here – the reunion with her parents imminent – she had to pull herself together. She could not re-enter this life looking as sick as she felt; she took deep breaths, hoping to suppress the desire to vomit the horrible, tasteless curry she'd had on the plane. She moved towards her parents without really seeing them. She thought she saw her father's full head of greying hair towering over most of the people, then suddenly he disappeared and she sensed that her mother was close by because she smelled her oppressive perfume, the one she had always worn since Ruthie could remember. Then her mother appeared, trim as ever, black wrap dress, shiny dark brown hair cut just above the shoulders, deep wine lipstick on her light macadamia-coloured skin (all the women on her mother's side had this colour, except Ruthie herself who was darker) moistened with her Lancôme, not a blemish, still looking lovely, even in her late forties.

"Sweetie, let me take that," she said, kissing both of Ruthie's cheeks, relieving Ruthie of her carry-on bag before she had a chance to respond, looking carefully at her daughter's face for any signs of mental instability.

"Taxi, Miss?" An Indian taxi driver hovered, repeating the question.

"No, no, thank you, we have a car." Mrs. B replied curtly. Where the hell was Charles? "How was the trip? Your father must have spotted you and gone to bring the car around. I never understand how he just disappears like that without saying a word…"

Her mother continued to talk, complaining about her father's disappearing acts; Ruthie didn't really focus on what she was saying. She was used to her mother's nervous chatter; it was always her way of dealing with uncomfortable situations, and this was obviously one. Ruthie's nausea had passed for the moment, but it was replaced by a lightheaded feeling, even a lightness of being, allowing her to float above the entire scene; she looked down on an amazing aerial view of the airport, the people, the cars and the highway leading into the lights of Port-of-Spain. She could even see the Stollmeyer's Castle facing the Queen's Park Savannah, the Queen's Royal College, the Archbishop's residence, but then she fell and landed right back on the pavement at the airport in front of her mother, suddenly very aware that she had left Boston and her Professor.

★

Mrs. B, who'd had to cultivate her elegance, studying her mother Simone's style very closely, simply did not understand how someone blessed with a long slim torso, ballerina legs, and such a graceful neck simply refused to acknowledge or take advantage of her good fortune. What a waste of a waist was all Mrs. B could think of as she examined her daughter's travelling attire. Ruthie looked so careless in the way she presented herself to the world – the untidiness of her adopted American lifestyle, the horrible hemp bag; that messy American-ness had become part of her look and it irritated Mrs. B. She didn't see herself as old fashioned, she'd had to accept the notion of being middle-aged, but what was wrong with wanting to present oneself in the best way possible. "Elegance," her mother Simone would say, "is the best defence." Mrs. B was well aware of how little elegance mattered to Charles, but she still strove for it and now she had to admit that for Ruthie, like her father, it didn't matter.

★

Seeing Ruthie again and remembering all that she had been through in April took Mrs. B back to another sad time in her life, of another arrival coupled with a departure. It was when Mrs. B was a young girl of eight going on nine, when she was called Marie Elena Roumain. In those days she played a game with God. It came to be called the Ceiling Game. The game started soon after she moved into her Aunt Claire's three-bedroom bungalow, in an area where all the houses looked the same – a box with a grey galvanized roof, a low white front wall, neatly potted plants that lined a short, narrow driveway that led to a narrower door into a small kitchen, just off the garage. Aunt Claire's small garden was no different from the others, except for the two swans and the white ceramic mother duck with four white ducklings that she had carefully placed just below the grotto that housed Mary, Joseph, baby Jesus, two oxen and three wise men. Marie Elena's mother, her Aunt Claire's one and only sister, Simone, used to say: "Clarita sweetie, I love you to death but I swear to God I think you may actually have the worst taste in the world." Then she would laugh, because from birth Simone had been given a powerful yet playful laugh; it gave her a free pass to speak her mind, saying exactly what she felt, when she felt it, seldom caring or even noticing who she slashed along the way. At the time, Marie Elena, the young Mrs. B, had not yet felt her mother's sting, but she had sensed that Aunt Claire avoided her sister as much as possible.

Her parents left the eight-year-old Marie Elena at Aunt Claire's house for two years. There were visits during those two years, and vacations when Elena would spend a month here with her father, Michael, or there with Simone. Sometimes Elena travelled to big cities like London or New York or other islands like Grenada, Jamaica, St Thomas or Barbuda; sometimes she spent weeks in a fancy hotel, and hours on planes being sent from the father to the mother, parcelled over from one air hostess to another. But after all those trips here, there and everywhere, Marie Elena would end up in the house on Hibiscus Drive with Auntie Claire.

Under her bed in an old shoe box where she was supposed to keep her white shoes for Sunday mass, Marie Elena put her mementos from her travels: postcards of couples lying on Grand Anse beach in Grenada; palm trees and sunsets in St Lucia; tiny shells from Martinique; a dime and a quarter snatched from a saucer; a pound note pressed in her palm by a stranger; a miniature Statue of Liberty, a tiny bright red double-decker bus, museum tickets, and the cap of the Coca Cola bottle from the day she shared a gigantic hot dog and two Cokes with her mother, sitting on a bench in Central Park. Marie Elena tried to collect memories as well, but these faded fast. So, from an early age, the future Mrs. B learned to hide what she treasured most.

There were times when Elena got very angry, berated her little self for what she should have remembered. In the days and months after her parents left her at Auntie Claire's, she often tried to recall the details of the morning they brought her to the house on Hibiscus Drive. Sometimes she saw her mother dressed up, laughing her strange, crazy, powerful laugh; sometimes she thought she saw her mother shed a tear; sometimes she saw her father in a dark suit trying his best not to look at her as he put down boxes of books, dolls and clothes in the tiny bedroom; sometimes she thought she saw her father smile. She thought she remembered her aunt standing like a thin, tall statue, barely breathing, holding her hand. When her parents drove away Elena remembered thinking that this would be the saddest part of her life, but she soon learned that life had many more days like this to offer.

In those days Marie Elena dreamed night and day of owning a city that was both island and metropolis, a big-city city like the ones she had visited with her parents. In these reveries she wasn't just owner of the city, keeper of the keys, lady at the gate, she, Elena, *was* the city. Powerful enough to change a building and become a building herself, she could also become a hurricane, a landslide, topple people from buildings with an earthquake, kill an entire village with a tidal wave. She drew a world filled with countries called ELENA on the pages of old copy books. There were ELENA cities with towering skyscrapers, ELENA villages with houses floating on rivers, ELENA oceans with fleets of ships – places drawn over sums and spelling tests. Sometimes she would glue old newspaper cuttings over the drawings, stick on beads or pieces of old cloth. Other times she would take leaves from the bougainvillea and flowers from the hibiscus and glue them into her world. Inspired by the *Alice in Wonderland* pop-up book her mother had given her, Elena tried to make her world like Alice's and for a while she was quite proud of what she had created. But even as God of her own world, with the power to build and destroy houses and families at will, her powers seemed to disappear when it came to her parents, so eventually Elena moved on to other things.

One of these was a promising friendship with God and his family. In church she had heard that everyone had a friend in

Jesus, so Elena saw no reason why she and God, Jesus's father, couldn't be friends, and if Jesus was God and God was Jesus and the Father was the Son and the Holy Spirit, she really didn't see a problem, the more the merrier. At eight years old, Elena got along very well with the Trinity, especially when they played games like the Ceiling Game. The rules were quite simple. If Elena managed to touch the ceiling in the hallway three times in a row, God or Jesus would have to grant her three wishes since three seemed to be their favourite number. Her strategy was usually to run as fast as she could, often without shoes (which she thought would make her lighter) stretch her arms above her head, and launch herself into the air, hoping that the tips of her fingers would graze the ceiling.

The ceiling wasn't that high but she had yet to grow into the long, slender body she would inherit from Michael and Simone. She often succeeded in touching the ceiling twice in a row, but never quite made three times, at least this is what she remembered. Sometimes Aunt Claire would catch her at this game and in her quiet, gentle way would say that Elena should not run in the hallway since she could have a bad fall. Most of the time, Claire left Elena to her own devices. At that age, the young Mrs. B pretended to be as good as any other eight year old girl; she did her homework, made her bed, had good table manners, always said please, thank you, good morning and you're welcome, went to piano lessons, did not fidget during Sunday morning Mass and always sat like a young lady. There was little for Aunt Claire to complain about.

Apart from the short vacations with her father or her mother, Elena lived in the house on Hibiscus Drive. Two years passed before she left her aunt to live mainly with her mother and occasionally with her father. By then, she had already fallen out in a big way with God, Jesus and the whole entourage. They with all their supreme powers, apparently could not protect her from a witch at school called Veronica and her young *sorcière* assistant, Monica, from a music teacher and from another creature whom Elena always kept nameless since he was nothing less than the devil on earth. With no God listening to her and monsters everywhere, her cities fell apart, and her powers began to fade like the old curtains in her Aunt Claire's drawing room. Great expectations began to drip, drip, drip like the leaking tap at the back of her Aunt Claire's house and she blamed everyone, but mostly her old friend God for all the leakage.

★

Aunt Claire was tall and thin, with the same macadamia-coloured skin as her sister. She was not glamorous, not as startlingly beautiful as Simone. If you ignored her slightly slanted, ink-coloured eyes, or the wideness of her smile, you might even think her pleasantly plain. It was true that she did not have the best taste when it came to what she wore or the furniture in her home; everything was functional, practical, neat and clean. She had lived alone for some years before her niece arrived, so perhaps she did not realize (or perhaps no longer cared) how plain she looked and how unadorned and simple her life had become. Everything had a place and there was a place for everything. She had folded and stacked her past carefully, leaving just a few spaces to slot in the future; her days were measured by ritual and routine: her morning ablutions, her prayers, her daily walk, her voluntary work at the church, her teaching and always her reading in the evening. It was this routine that made her sister Simone say that Elena would be a gift, a blessing to "poor, lonely Claire", that her existence would suddenly have purpose and meaning. Simone was tempted to think "old maid", but she resisted; Claire at thirty-three was only two years her senior.

Truth be told, Claire did not want to take care of Elena. She had no desire to raise a child – those painful feelings had long passed. But she was never as powerful as Simone, even though she was the elder; and though she thought she had shown outward signs of protest, Simone pretended not to notice. Simone drew her older sister in with all her charms, hypnotizing her with her sorrows, dangling the precious spirits of their dead parents and even speaking for them. "Wouldn't they have wanted their grand-daughter to have a peaceful place during these stormy times," and then promising that Elena would only be there for a couple of months, not the two years that she had probably intended all along. It was not that Claire was weak with everyone; she had stood up to seemingly greater forces than her sister, but for reasons that she did not understand, Simone had managed to manipulate her ever since she could speak. Simone knew this and knew that Claire knew she knew this. The rules of the game had never changed.

★

During the day Claire was known simply as "Miss" to her third standard class at the Princess Margaret Primary School, conveniently located within walking distance from 623 Hibiscus Drive, where she had moved two years before Elena's arrival. Claire had tried her best to find complete contentment in her teaching, trying to live for those little brown, third-standard faces that looked to their "Miss" for all the answers, but she had to admit that it was not enough and at times tremendously tedious. She would have preferred to spend her day in the room she called her library. A librarian was what she had dreamed of becoming – she had never wanted to be a teacher, but without the necessary qualifications she had been forced to settle for the job of "Miss". As a librarian there would be fewer questions, definitely less noise and no more Miss. There would be no need to make small talk with the other teachers; she imagined all librarians sought the same solitude. She could barely control her ecstasy when she imagined herself surrounded by shelves and shelves of books; there was something she found on the second floor of the Port of Spain Public Library that she could not find even in church. But there was also the guilt that she felt at the thought of reading her favourite poems with Mary, Jesus and all the saints looking over her shoulder, and she had never missed Sunday Mass even though there were days when the early morning rain made her feel like lying in bed with Baudelaire. To others, Claire's love of reading did not seem to go beyond the obvious – a romantic to the core, it allowed her to escape to another world, to be transported from an ordinary life to something better. It gave her the simple pleasure of being lost, of never noticing time passing because, more than anything, Claire wanted time to pass. She believed all the clichés about wounds being healed by the balm of time. Sometimes, though, Claire read in a way that others were less likely to deduce; sometimes what she felt could only be described as a *frisson*: discovering new words or following the patterns that the sentences made, seeing beauty in simplicity, complexity in that beauty, perfection in all its forms and shapes – page after page. Claire loved it all – no, it was more than love – it was pure adoration. There was another gratifying aspect to her reading; it was the only advantage, although slight, that she had over Simone, who had never been much of a reader.

As a child, Claire, like her father (another great reader, and the one who taught her, more than any teacher, how to read), read all the time, though her family was not sure that it was the best thing for someone as homely looking as Claire to fill her mind with false hopes and the Cinderella expectations that these books might give. Her old aunts feared that Claire would further lessen her chances of finding a good husband if her vocabulary continued to expand at such a quick pace. No man wanted a wife who seemed more intelligent than he. The old aunts lived in a perpetual state of anxiety about poor Claire's future. It didn't help when two Fathers of the parish came to the house one afternoon to have tea with the Roumain family that Claire was seen holding a Koran, (taken from her father's library). Needless to say, the priests noticed, mentioned it to the old aunts, who in turn encouraged Claire's father to be a little more vigilant about his daughter's choice of reading material.

Indeed, the old aunts strongly urged Claire's parents to censor her selection of books. Until then, Claire had been allowed to browse the shelves and select at will novels, poetry, plays, books on horticulture, agriculture, bird-watching, fishing and the history of the British Empire. Her parents had already removed unsuitable texts like the *Kama Sutra*, the Marquis de Sade and the banned poems of Baudelaire. After the Koran incident and the old aunts' insidious nagging, a battle for righteousness, though not the war, was won. For a while it was salvation over education.

As a young girl, Claire also read to hide behind a book, shying away from questions, requests and social gatherings. Unlike Simone, who shone like a jewel in a crowd, Claire wanted to disappear. In those days Claire's books were her only shields, though she learned that they could not protect her from the disappointment of a missed party because her family did not know the parents of the little girl or boy she liked, and they certainly could not protect her from the pain that an aunt or an uncle inflicted so casually with a cruel word or careless remark.

In her study, Claire arranged her books the way she wished she could have arranged her past life – carefully, thoughtfully, even with kindness, making sure that those with similar ideas, religious beliefs or experiences were grouped together; some kind of correspondence had to take place on her shelves. So instead of putting *Madame Bovary* with all the other 19th century French novels she had collected during her year in Paris, she thought that Emma should be next to Anna Karenina. With so much pain to share, the two women could comfort each other. Verlaine and Rimbaud, having endured such violent quarrels, could never be next to each other, so she put Rimbaud next to Ronsard, and Verlaine next to Watteau, a painter he admired. Baudelaire stayed away from Hugo and was placed next to another great, Shakespeare. Even if the two men were from different times Claire felt that they shared dark loves and battles of the soul.

But there was more; while reading shielded her from the outside, familiarity with her books guided her into other places. What Claire loved most was that she knew what to expect, she knew the plots by heart; there were no surprises. Claire could drop in and out, just like Alice in Wonderland; she could assume different roles at different parts of different books; she could become the heroine in one chapter or a less important character in another. It was ridiculous how many times she had reread *Madame Bovary*; just holding that book could take her into the back of the carriage with Leon or into the woods with Rodolphe. She knew what the kiss did to Emma. Claire could almost feel it, and once she actually held the page close to her lips that were parted ever so slightly, just the way she imagined Emma's had been with Rodolphe that afternoon. Claire knew Emma better than any other character because in her own life she had met her own Leon and several Rodolphes.

What no-one knew about Claire's reading was that the more times she read a book, the more emboldened she was to take liberties with the writer's decisions; sometimes she would scribble passages in her notebook that changed the plots or parts of the story. She would have allowed Emma to be consoled by a kind priest, not the uncaring one in the book, but a new, charming character, who when Emma went into the church that day seeking guidance or some sort of solace, would seduce Emma back into the church with his intelligence, heightened sensibility and overpowering good looks.

Claire knew that the family was not happy that she lived alone, but it was the only way she could survive the brutalities committed against her so early on. She knew this aloneness made her seem a little odd, and even she wondered if living in these fantasies was a sign of some abnormality, but was she hurting anyone? And did anyone really care what she did with her time? So she enjoyed her invisibility more and more and kept these imaginings to herself. Everyone had secrets, even Simone.

So imagine Elena's surprise the day she walked into Aunt Claire's study for the first time. The small room was filled with books on every wall save one where there was a sofa, a lamp and two votives on a side table. The room had a strange smell; a mixture of hot chocolate, vetiver, vanilla and something else. It was a male smell.

# CHAPTER TWO
## HOME SWEET HOME

Mrs. B had spent a lot of time, energy and money refurbishing the guest room for Ruthie's arrival. She wanted Ruthie to have more space, more privacy and the guest room downstairs had a private bathroom. She knew that Ruthie didn't like their new home in a gated community, the San Pedro Villas. In fact neither Mrs. B nor Charles had really become used to it; there were too many neighbours, too much gossip. They had never wanted to leave their five-acre home in the valley. Mrs. B still missed the white egrets on the lawn in the morning, the parrots flying home to the bamboo trees in the evening and their mini estate of oranges, grapefruits, avocados, mangoes and lime trees. In their last years in the valley, Mrs. B and her longtime gardener, Sammy, had grown a healthy kitchen garden of basil, thyme, rosemary and mint just off the kitchen porch. Only the herb garden had been transplanted, but now clay pots held the plants and the roots were no longer in the earth.

Their house in the valley had a verandah built to imitate the old colonial style; it wrapped around most of the ground floor and allowed an easy flow onto the soft Bermuda grass. Before Charles and Mrs. B built the house she had wanted to buy one of the older colonial estate homes, like the ones her family owned when she was a child, but Charles said this was impractical since restoring the homes she liked would have cost as much as constructing a new one. But she had managed, with Charles and their architect, to build a home with all the nostalgic details of her childhood: high wooden ceilings, tall doors, and wooden latticework along the edges of the roof.

During her first few months in San Pedro she had enjoyed the company of her neighbours – many of whom they knew from high school days – and the ability to see her close friends, who all lived nearby. But after a while she began to miss the things she had taken for granted in her old home; here in San Pedro the constant need to meet, greet and give daily updates on anything and everything began to irritate. A face seemed to appear the moment she stepped out of her townhouse door, or out of her car, or even when she sought some peace in her small backyard garden. In San Pedro, the custom of phoning before a visit seemed unnecessary especially since the neighbour lived only minutes away; walking in to someone's front door and simply calling out "Hello" was the norm. After four years Mrs. B had grown tired of the place; she longed for the simple pleasure of walking to the edge of her old property and sitting on her favourite bench under the sprawling samaan tree just above the path that led down to the river.

Originally San Pedro seemed the best option: good location in the west, excellent neighbourhood, mall and grocery minutes away, with a view of the sea. Each unit had three bedrooms, three bathrooms and a powder room, a living area to the back that opened onto a small but thoughtfully landscaped garden with neat beds of ginger lilies, alamandas, and exotic ground cover. There were some tall, carefully pruned ficus and a few weeping willows at the edge of the compound. Separating side A from side B of the compound were nine royal palms that gave it an air of grandeur. It was the palms that had drawn Mrs. B and Charles to San Pedro.

But she couldn't help making comparisons with the valley. On mornings in San Pedro, young twenty-something housewives left their babies with housekeepers who arrived in droves at the crack of dawn as their young employers went to work or the gym in their shiny new cars. In the afternoons Mrs. B would see the mothers once again, walking their little cherubs in fancy carriages around the compound. The fathers would come home in the evening, suited and tired. The sight of the young families affected Mrs. B with envy, nostalgia and an indescribable numbness. Besides the young couples, there were many like Mrs. B and Charles, a group of forty-somethings to fifty-somethings who had left much larger properties partly for the convenience but primarily for the security. San Pedro boasted the best guarded gated community in the west; whether this was true or not, it didn't hurt that the family of one of the young Lebanese couples living there owned the security firm that guarded the compound. At night, guards patrolled with pit bulls; they were without them during the day, but always carried concealed weapons. Curled barbed wire atop the compound walls bordering the main street mostly deterred bandits from jumping over, though the previous Carnival season, two crackheads, or *pipers*, hazarded a jump, only to be welcomed by pit bulls, guns, batons and cricket bats.

At first, Mrs. B and Charles resisted the temptation to spend their early evenings discussing the crime situation with their neighbours. They thought they had left fear behind in the valley, along with the surplus goods donated to Goodwill, the Red Cross and Salvation Army, or given to the local valley poor, but even in the guarded compound the wives spoke about robberies, rapes, murders and kidnappings all the time, and Mrs. B and Charles soon discovered that fear was not something you left behind or gave away, like an old pair of shoes.

Still, in spite of the nostalgia she felt, Mrs. B had to admit that her valley, like everything else on the island, had changed. In recent years those who had made Coco Valley their home had built towering walls that locked them in, making sure that the villagers who walked past had no chance of seeing anything inside their palaces. But with each robbery that took place in the valley, each kidnapping, each shooting, Mrs. B and Charles felt the enemy was getting too close. At night every pop became a gunshot. Then there was the body dumped in the canal by the main road that snaked through the valley, bloating in the sun like a dead dog. Life in Coco Valley had ceased to exist in the way they wanted to remember it. There was no one to call on to protect and serve them. "Not one jackass," Charles would say in his diatribes against the corrupt police force and even more corrupt politicians – many of whom, as he claimed, enjoyed the profits of a healthy drug trade. It was better for witnesses to pretend to know nothing, because witnesses were shot all the time, even on the steps of the Hall of Justice.

When they first moved into Coco Valley things were different. There were more trees, more bush, more shades of green; there were fewer houses, more cocoa plantations, fewer cars, more villagers on bikes; it was less town and more country, and that was what Mrs. B and Charles had loved. Although they were not born in the valley, they felt that the almost two decades they spent there earned them the right to feel that they belonged. Ruthie had grown up in the valley; she knew no other home.

When the horrors began, Mrs. B and Charles pretended not to notice. They were not unique to Coco Valley; evil things were taking place all over the island. Like many of their friends, Mrs. B and Charles went about their daily routines trying hard not to think about the way things were falling apart. They busied themselves with shopping at the malls, doing their groceries on a Saturday morning, movies on a Sunday evening, dinners with friends, lunches, brunches – avoiding restaurants that had been held up by bandits; they had self-imposed curfews and travelled in numbers at night, never going into the city after dark, or never going into the city at all. When they got into their cars, day or night, they locked their doors, kept their windows up, air conditioners on; looked closely as their electric gates opened and closed behind them; let their dogs out at night and hired security to patrol their neighbourhood. That was the way they survived, skimming the surface of a deep red sea, never looking down to see what was below.

But then there was the incident with Mary, their neighbour in the valley. She lived with her handsome husband and her ten-year-old twin boys. The day began like any other: husband off to work, twins off to school, housekeeper housekeeping, gardener gardening. They arrived quietly, through the back gate that led to the river (they never found out who left it unlocked). The men knew the Rottweilers were tied up, and they found Mary where she spent every sunny morning in the valley, in her garden weeding, cleaning up a bed next to the tall African tulip. That was where they ripped her apart. Worse than raging pit bulls, they bit, tore, straddled, paddled, and broke Mary like a dry twig in her own garden. They ate the lunch the housekeeper had cooked for the family (she said she was kicked around before they locked her in the powder room at the bottom of the stairs, but compared to Miss Mary, she knew she had been spared). Before they left, they shat on the kitchen floor and used their excrement to write FOCK YOU across the white kitchen walls, and then they packed the laptops, the Wiis, the Xbox, the cell phones and the shoebox with Mary's jewellery and five thousand US into Mary's Mercedes and drove off into the bright valley light. The gardener, who had hidden in the shed outside, swore they had guns, swore that they threatened to kill him if he said anything to the police. Mary's husband Joey and their two young sons had to clean up the entire mess, not just the house but Mary herself, who never again felt clean.

After this, Mrs. B and Charles realized they had to leave.

★

Mrs. B was busy preparing the guest room for Ruthie. The idea that pleased her most was the motif of shells; she had chosen a shell-pattern curtain fabric at the ever popular "Jeanelle's" and gathered several conch shells that she had found with Charles on their last holiday in Tobago and put them on the book shelf. But it didn't end there; she asked her seamstress, Jeanelle's daughter Taneeka, to make a bedspread using the same fabric, and then to add a few cushions as well. Charles was sure that Ruthie would hate the shells, and painting the room pinkish-orange to match the curtains made him cringe; the whole idea was very un-Ruthie. But when it came to Ruthie, Charles always felt that his wife tried too hard, though he seldom contradicted her on things that mattered to her; he seldom contradicted her at all. During the two weeks before Ruthie's arrival, Charles would peep into the room to observe the progress. There, Mr. Kenny, housepainter-handyman, originally from a Hindu village in Coco Valley, with his son Ricky, was dusting, hanging curtains and painting. The room's colour looked like a perpetual sunset. Ruthie would loath it, but when Mr. Kenny asked, "How you like it, Mr. Charles?" he could only reply, "Looking good, man. I like the colour." Mr. Kenny looked pleased. "Yeah, it nice."

Charles saw how much Ruthie's breakdown had affected his wife; she acted as though she was somehow responsible for it. He knew that she wanted him to share in this responsibility, but when she came back from Boston, acting as though she had attended a funeral, he refused to walk around the house as if in mourning – though he could see how this was angering his wife. He had never demanded too much from his daughter. He missed her when she left for university, though they had never been very close and seldom shared their feelings with each other. Ruthie was not a talker and neither was he; they were both comfortable with silence. She had made few demands as a young girl and he was grateful for that because he would not have known how to respond. His father and grandfather belonged to that generation of Caribbean men who knew what they were supposed to do; there were areas they inhabited comfortably and others they quickly vacated. Now more was expected of a husband and a father and Charles just didn't know where and when he was supposed to be what. So even if he wanted to stroke Ruthie's hair or kiss her without the formality of a goodnight, goodbye or a good-morning, he simply couldn't; and if, as TV fathers did, he felt he should ask her about her day, the words would not come out. Yet he felt that he could read Ruthie better than his wife. She seemed to miss the details – the subtle shift in tone, the quick grimace, the way Ruthie opened her large eyes even wider when she was unhappy, and the pain she felt when her mother made her the focus of attention. At the parent-teacher conferences when Ruthie was at primary school, the school would say that Ruthie was a bright student, never giving any trouble in class, but they didn't think she was happy. She never seemed to want to play with the other children, and at break time she would sit quietly or simply stare at some fixed point. It hurt Charles to hear this, but it seemed not to bother his wife, because Ruthie, throughout primary and secondary school, was always in the top three of her class.

★

Although, even after two years of therapy, Mrs. B could only describe her feelings towards her mother as ambiguous, she had to admit that she admired Simone's air of quiet superiority. Charles saw no value in this. Sophistication and snobbery equalled hypocrisy in his mind. He liked people who were "down to earth"; he didn't like fakes or show-offs and he had never cared much for his mother-in-law; the feeling was mutual.

But during his courtship, Charles's rough, unpolished, earthy persona was exactly what the future Mrs. B found most enticing; in her young mind, he represented a revolution, something far away from what the family expected. She didn't want a lawyer or a doctor. But that was before time began to play tricks – shortening the good years, stretching the bad, making five good years feel like a week, and five bad, a lifetime.

They met when she was twenty, he twenty-two; by her twenty-first birthday she was married; by twenty-two Ruthie was in her arms. In the early days Charles courted, romanced, did all that was expected, but with each passing year there seemed less to talk about and by the time Ruthie went away, there was little left to share. Nothing she said or did brought a smile to his face; she tried to ignore the fact that Charles only seemed to laugh when he talked to his cricket buddies, his best friend Chow, or his brother on the phone, and that he was always happier when he came back from his Sunday morning walks around the Queen's Park Savannah with his old high-school cronies. His mood had clouded again by the time he had finished Sunday lunch, even his favourite of roasted lamb, macaroni pie, callaloo, stewed red beans with pumpkin, tomato, cucumber and lettuce salad with a vinaigrette dressing, followed by coconut ice-cream. There were times when, with the hope of a compliment from Charles, Mrs. B prepared dishes that they had eaten on their vacations in Milan, in Paris, or Madrid – dishes that Charles had eaten with such gusto in those foreign cities. At home, Charles seldom showed the same pleasure; he had said more than once that "something was missing". Mrs. B wasn't sure whether she had stopped telling Charles about her life before she realized that he had stopped telling her about his.

★

The day she left Boston for Trinidad, Ruthie dressed for what would be the last time in the small rent-controlled apartment in Cambridge. She had spent so much time sipping warm *café au laits* on crisp Cambridge afternoons in Harvard Square, watching the old men play chess while she waited for her Professor to finish his last lecture. When he appeared it always surprised her that this was her lover – this quintessential professor with his dark brown hair, blue eyes, tall, lanky body in loose Levis, tee shirt and his professor uniform of a rumpled corduroy jacket. Together they would walk casually to the apartment ten minutes away from the Square.

She knew she had spent too many afternoons in the last year in this apartment with her Professor; making love too many times on the dusty sofas, the Persian carpets, and the creaky four poster in the master bedroom. In the last month she had actually moved into the apartment, morning to night, lying to her parents, telling them it was shared with someone from her class. They believed her when she said that since the bathroom episode, she simply could not go back to face Alice and the others. This was not a complete lie. Those American friends, who had come to visit her when she was in the clinic bearing gifts and Hallmark greetings, saying how much they missed her, that it was not the same without her, were all liars. In the two years since Ruthie hooked up with her Professor, she had seldom slept in her dorm room and tried her best to distance herself from the other students; she never said much beyond the necessary civilities, fearing their suspicions and discovery of her secret life. It would have been impossible to see her Professor in the dorm; they knew who he was, not so much for his course on Pound and Eliot, but more for his gorgeous looks.

So when the Professor's friend and colleague in the Art History Department asked him to take care of his apartment by emptying the mail box, paying the bills, and watering the plants for a semester while he was in Florence, her Professor couldn't believe his luck. Her Professor swore, more than once, on his mother's grave, that this colleague did not know about the affair but Ruthie never believed him and even took some pleasure in the fact that someone knew; it made the whole affair seem real. But she knew she couldn't trust her Professor; she had heard him lie to his wife and daughter on the phone in his steady, calm unwavering tone while she strolled around the apartment in her skimpy panties and nothing else. She had heard him talk to a colleague while he fondled her nipples; he used the same tone in his lectures, the same one that had seduced her; he had said that his wife no longer cared about their marriage; that Ruthie was his first student-professor affair; that their love for each other was something extraordinary; that the heart has a mind of its own and that what they felt could not be ignored. Words came to him so cheaply. Sometimes it had bothered her.

The Art Historian's apartment added a new dimension to their trysts; they could play house, no more dirty-sexy hook-ups in posh hotels, or tacky motel rooms with huge mirrors, or bare-boned conference accommodation on some university campus. Since she met the Professor, Ruthie could feel the emptiness she'd felt ever since she was a little girl being replaced by a heady passion. And although Ruthie had mastered, at a very early age, the skill of detaching herself from people, places and things, the Professor found a way very slowly, and very gently, to guide her into places she'd refused to go to before she met him.

By the end of the first year of the affair, the Professor's wife seemed suspicious of her husband's renewed interest in presenting conference papers at this stage of his academic career. Her persistent interrogations, her insistence on knowing all the travel arrangements – studying his itinerary and conference details – began to take its toll and he was forced to cut back on these presentations. Then, just as things were beginning to look a little shaky, the opportunity to baby-sit the apartment presented itself. The Professor adopted a policy of transparency, telling his wife every detail about the apartment, especially since she went across the river to Cambridge at least twice a week to her favourite bookstore in Harvard Square. She even walked past the apartment a couple of times just to make sure that he was not there. Though she couldn't see inside, because the curtains were always drawn, there seemed to be no sign of her husband or his car, so she had to conclude that perhaps she could believe what he had said. There was also the fact that the Art History professor was gay. He was discreet but not closeted, and perhaps the Professor's wife thought that the flat was immune from heterosexual affairs having been infused with its owner's gayness – or perhaps she had decided that discovery was sometimes worse than doubt.

★

If ever she was going to make an effort to look her best, Ruthie knew this should be the time – except she lacked the energy and will to get beyond the debilitating fatigue that made it difficult to even think about an outfit for the plane, more so one that would

32

meet her mother's approval. Apart from the clear gloss she spread on her lips and the black eyeliner, she wore no other make-up on her faded skin, normally much browner when she was at home. She put her unwashed oily hair into a loose bun, knowing that once she stepped out of the plane into the humid island air, her hair would be a mess anyway. She slipped into a pair of her favourite Old Navy jeans; this last month she had lost even more weight (perhaps her mother would appreciate this – "never too rich or too thin") but when she looked in the mirror she saw a gaunt, drawn, unattractive face. The only things left out of the big black suitcase were a white tank top, a black cardigan and a pair of old black ballerina flats. Two suitcases and a knapsack with her laptop and her hemp bag were all she had. Everything else had been sent home; the Professor and Eddy had helped her with this. She had packed up four years in a few days: books, linens, tokens she had collected over the years in Boston or on her brief trips to Europe. She had come to Boston alone and was leaving alone.

It was an early flight from Logan to JFK, where Ruthie would connect to Miami, then Barbados and finally home. She was supposed to have left her keys to the Cambridge apartment on the coffee table in the living room but she hadn't; her Professor had left two days earlier for a conveniently timed vacation with his wife and daughter in London. Their last afternoon together in the apartment had been a disaster. They drove to Walden Pond; he spoke about Thoreau and a recent annotated edition; she had heard this little lecture before. When they got back to the apartment after dinner at their favourite Indian restaurant in Kenmore Square, she broke her promise to herself and had sex with him, the hungry kind that you have when you think it may be the last time. As soon as he left she felt sick, nauseous and broken. When she was in the clinic earlier that April, after his quick, nervous visit she swore on her father's life that she would never see him again, but her Professor was stronger than any drug she had ever tried, though she knew she was not his first student, even before he confessed. Before she left the apartment she decided, uncharacteristically, to keep the keys as a token, not expecting to ever return but simply to have some proof of it all.

★

"There he is. Let's hope he doesn't drive past us." Mrs. B waved to her husband who was luckily able to draw up just in front of where they were standing. Charles had not seen his daughter since January; he found he could barely look at her. He got out and moved towards her, kissing both cheeks and felt her hair brushing against his face. She looked thin, tired but still so pretty, always his little girl. He could see that she was anxious and that worried him; but they were all nervous about this return.

The moment Ruthie saw her father and the familiar unhappiness on his face, the sadness came back and it took her by surprise. She had managed to fill herself with anger and anxiety on the plane, fuelled by thoughts of the Professor's abandonment and the inevitable disapproval and disappointment she would have to face from her mother and the family. But sadness and longing – she was unprepared for this and it left her weak.

Little was said on the drive home. Ruthie did notice the new car and told her father how comfortable it was. Her mother only reported on what she thought was necessary – news about friends Ruthie no longer cared about and the possibility of a job at *The Guardian* or *The Express* as soon as she felt up to it, but obviously there was no rush. The rest was just ramblings about the escalating crime, the corruption, the President; it allowed Ruthie to tune in and out as she had always done with her mother. How easily these tricks came back to her, feigning attention to the details piled upon details. Her father usually tried to protect her from the plans her mother made to show her off, but Ruthie soon realized that unlike previous returns where her mother would have planned a million little lunches, brunches and dinners, nothing was being said about anything like this. Rest was what her mother said she needed; it was clear to Ruthie that her mother didn't think she was ready to be presented to friends or family.

They passed the turn-off that would have taken them to their old home in the valley. Ruthie suddenly thought of her dogs, how she and her father would take them for walks in the trails leading to the hills behind the house. On Saturdays, Ruthie would help her father bathe them, and then tie them in a sunny spot to dry. They had enrolled the two German shepherds, Thena and Pollo, in training classes, and even entered them in a couple of dog shows. Ruthie had watched her father and their gardener bury both dogs in the backyard near to one of the poui trees; the dogs had died of old age within months of each other. There had always been at least five dogs on the property at any given time. Left to Ruthie there would have been ten but her mother didn't like dogs and only tolerated them because of the security they provided and because, as she acknowledged, Ruthie and Charles were "dog people".

Her father drove through the imposing electric gates of San Pedro, waving to the security guards, and parked his vehicle next to her mother's. Her parents carried her bags in for her as if she was an invalid. Every year her mother had tried to make it look more and more like a reduced version of their valley home; there were all their paintings, their vases, their photographs, the inherited antiques and their rugs. As she entered Ruthie thought about the poem her Professor had recited to her early in the courtship. She had even tried to memorize it; it went something like, "The time will come when, with elation, you will greet yourself arriving at your own door, in your own mirror, and each will smile at the other's welcome." There was more but that was all she could remember.

But Ruthie did not know how to greet this self arriving at her door; she had changed so much in the last few years that she no longer recognized the person in the antique mirror from the old valley house. She had no idea how to welcome this new self or to introduce it to the old one, and the promise of elation was not something she expected as she walked into this home. Home. Already she could feel it; all the things she wanted to leave behind were still waiting right there for her.

Ruthie did not like the refurbished guest room; she preferred it the way it was before, when they first moved in, bare and white. She would have preferred her room upstairs, the one her mother said was hers. And yet the minute her mother opened the door and her father put her suitcases on the new sisal mat, she thanked her parents, especially her mother, for everything they had done and for the room.

"It's lovely, Mummy, thank you," Ruthie said.

"And your father was worried that you wouldn't like it." Mrs. B turned and gave Charles a self-satisfied glance.

"We'll let you get organized and I'll make a little something for you to eat." Mrs. B rested her hand awkwardly on her daughter's arm.

Ruthie didn't unpack right away; instead she lay on her bed and stared at the ceiling. The bright colours really didn't help, they seemed to magnify how uncomfortable she felt, but perhaps this was the best place for her, the most appropriate room to occupy, for she *was* a guest in this house, as she felt like a guest in her own body. What she had failed to do in Boston flashed through her mind as quickly as her Professor reappeared. "There will be no more of that," he had said at the clinic the night after her mother left, "No more of that."

She lay on the bedspread of shells waiting for her mother to call her; the ritual of return from the airport demanded that she have a chicken salad sandwich on wholewheat bread with grapefruit juice or a glass of white wine – now that she was "no longer a child." Chicken salad had been her favourite when she was a little girl and her mother always had their Grenadian housekeeper of a million years, Miss Milly, make it the first meal Ruthie had when she came home. So, at eleven o'clock at night, Ruthie found herself sitting at the long, oiled teak table eating a sandwich that she could barely keep down. Her father ate in his usual mechanical manner, staring at nothing in particular; her mother sipped her glass of chilled white wine and tried not to look at Charles while he ate. Only in the last few years had Mrs. B admitted to herself how much his bovine chewing irritated her.

"Tomorrow you should just rest," Mrs. B said, "unless you want to go to the pool."

"Anything is fine, but maybe I'll just take it easy," Ruthie said. "I am a little tired."

"You must be, after such a hard semester." The moment Mrs. B said this she regretted it. But Ruthie said nothing, neither did Charles.

Although the compound had a pool, Ruthie preferred not to swim within view of her San Pedro neighbours. She missed the privacy of their life in the valley, their private pool, their lawns at the back and front of the house, their view of the hills surrounding them, protecting them. When her parents moved into this gated community, she decided to take up membership at a nearby hotel, which gave her access to its pool, tennis courts and, more importantly, time away from this communal living. Ruthie understood her parents' need to be safe; the country was in a mess with a few monsters terrorizing many, making their victims live behind burglar bars like prisoners while they roamed free. Some of the families she knew had been through nightmares of kidnappings, rapes and even murder; a friend's uncle had been stabbed fifteen times by a sixteen year old boy trying to rob the store; another boy who she knew from primary school had been kidnapped – although he told the newspapers that the kidnappers treated him well, serving him Chinese food and nut cakes for the week until his father paid the ransom of one million US dollars. The stories went on without end. The place, Ruthie thought, had grown as ugly as she felt.

Before she went to bed her father poked his head through the door.

"Goodnight, my beauty. Happy to have you back home," he said.

"Yes, so am I, I mean happy to be back home. Thanks for everything, Daddy." Ruthie got off the bed where she had been sitting and kissed him goodnight on his cheek; it was damp but smooth with the scent of his woodsy aftershave. He had obviously shaved before coming to meet her at the airport.

Her mother called from upstairs, "Sleep well, my darling," but she didn't come down.

"Goodnight, Mum, thanks for everything."

Return complete, mission accomplished, but Ruthie did not sleep well. She tried to read, got up for a drink of water, turned off the bedside lamp yet again, but still she felt uncomfortable, hot then cold, but mostly she felt terribly alone.

# CHAPTER THREE
## BAD BEHAVIOUR

In July of 1990 there were two coups in Mrs. B's life: the first was private and the second public. The first a *coup de foudre,* the second a *coup d'état*. Neither attempt – to overthrow respectively a life and a government – was successful, but there were losses on both sides. To this day, Mrs. B remembers exactly where she was on the afternoon of July 27th when her husband called; she was lying on rumpled bed covers with her bedroom curtains partially drawn, still sweetly drowsy, still naked with a sheet pulled partially over her neat breasts and flat torso to reveal her long, slim legs. Only moments before the telephone call, Mrs. B had been kissed on the back of her neck by her lover of exactly three months, Larry Blackburn, known to all of his friends, including her husband, as Chow.

The news from Charles was fast, telegraphic: he wasn't at the football match, Muslimeen were in the Red House, hostages held in the parliament, people shot, Police Headquarters blown up, the city was a mess, fires, looting, coming home right away. "Don't panic," he told her, "just stay right there with Ruthie." But she did panic. Ruthie wasn't there with her, she had left her with Charles's mother, Naomi. The afternoon rendezvous had been carefully planned. Charles would be at the football match with the rest of the country, Ruthie with her granny Naomi, giving Larry and her at least two hours of delicious play. Out of disbelief, but also for Larry's benefit, she had repeated word for word what her husband had been saying. Without a minute to waste, faster than any superhero, Larry leapt out of bed, dressed, and was waiting for her to hang up so he could call his wife, Rachel, who was also supposed to have been at the football match with some of her girlfriends. These were not the days when every man, woman and child on the island had a cell phone, so Larry had to make his call on the land line. No reply. Naturally, the line was busy. Then he turned on the television and the radio, as if they would let him know where his wife was. Meantime, Mrs. B had also dressed and simply couldn't wait for Larry to leave. Minutes ago the thought of the afternoon coming to an end had almost brought tears to her eyes, but now she just wanted him to disappear and Ruthie to be at home. The next phone call was to her mother-in-law, Naomi. The line was busy.

Larry left. Mrs. B got into her car and drove over to Naomi who lived just over the hill about thirty minutes away, but as she drove out of the valley, into more inhabited neighbourhoods, finally onto the main road and turn-off at the road that would take her over the hill, she started to panic again. She didn't want Charles to get home before she did, fearing that he would suspect something, or find some piece of evidence linking her to Larry. She had to get to Ruthie. But the roads were already a mess; there was crawling traffic near to the gas stations where people were trying to fill up their tanks. Cars were parked almost in the middle of the street; people were pushing their way into the smaller grocers since the big grocery chains had already shut their doors. Mrs. B felt herself breathing faster; all she could think about was Ruthie's little face.

As Mrs. B turned into Naomi's quiet neighbourhood and drove up the wide, smooth, asphalt avenue, the neighbours were gathered at their gates, talking over walls, each conversation adding another line to the last sentence, making the stories longer, changing fact to fiction, truth to rumour, prescience to clairvoyance, portending and predicting the drama to come.

Naomi was not at her gate; she was inside with Ruthie, waiting for her son or daughter-in-law to arrive. Ruthie's bag was already packed with the dress she came in, her favourite toy, her book and a snack. Naomi was sitting in the living room with Ruthie on her lap. Ruthie had been a quiet baby and was a quiet child, but very articulate when she did speak, alert but undemanding, independent but not unaffectionate, and very unaware of the pretty four year old she then was. If her Granny Simone ignored her, her

Granny Naomi adored her, though Ruthie was not her first grandchild, and Mrs. B had not been Naomi's first choice for her son. But then, Charles was not an overly thoughtful son, unlike his brother Robby, who visited or called his mother almost every day. Still, Naomi saw something in Ruthie that she could not put into words; she had simply fallen in love with the little girl from the day she was born and that was that.

Mrs. B parked the car, opened the gate, pushed away the dogs and ran into the house. She knew she didn't have much time before she fell apart; she had to get Ruthie home as fast as she could. She thanked Naomi, almost forgot Ruthie's bag, and only remembered to ask at the door whether Naomi would be alright, or did she want to come to their home.

"Robby is coming soon," Naomi said, underlining the fact that Charles and his wife were not the most attentive family members, even after Naomi had become a widow, losing Charles's father to cancer two years before. But Mrs. B, frequently irritated by these tangential attacks, barely registered what Naomi said.

"This is terrible, all of this," Mrs. B said as she picked up Ruthie.

"She hasn't eaten much but I managed to give her a bath before all of this drama." Naomi gave Ruthie another kiss. "You didn't have much to eat did you, sweetie pie? Just a little snack, so she'll be hungry."

Mrs. B was strapping Ruthie into the car seat, when Naomi asked about Charles.

"On his way," Mrs. B replied as she got into the car, then suddenly remembered her manners. "Thank you, Naomi. Tell Granny Omi bye-bye. Are you sure you'll be okay?" Naomi nodded, and Mrs. B drove off, disappearing almost as fast as Larry had earlier.

★

At around 6 pm, Mrs. B and Charles sat staring at the TV screen. Ruthie had fallen asleep on the sofa, her head on her mother's lap. The lamp in the living room was the only source of light; plates with leftover pieces of the cheese omelettes they had eaten for dinner were still on the coffee table. The phone that had been ringing constantly suddenly stopped. They were all listening, the entire nation. The coup leader had the attention of the people as he made his case, promising to be their saviour, their prophet Mohammed and their Moses, ready to lead his people to the promised land.

"This had to happen; they let him set up his compound, and his army and now we all have to pay. They need to go in there and just shoot his ass!" Charles blamed the present government, the Americans, the British. Everyone was responsible, no one escaped his wrath. Mrs. B had been looking at the TV screen as though she were viewing a film; the leader was sitting there in his white Muslim garb, glancing at his script, then looking directly into the camera. She listened but her mind kept going back to earlier that afternoon and how fast Larry had left her when he heard the news. She wasn't sure whether she was angrier with the coup leader or Larry. His loyalty to his wife was expected but his cowardly desertion was not. She forgot that she had actually wanted him to leave after she got the call from Charles. But Larry hadn't even tried to call her, not once. Mrs. B's thoughts began to avalanche. Larry, his wife, his spoiled children and Charles: they were all responsible in some way. Charles was still ranting at the TV screen; Mrs. B thought this made him look cowardly, desperate – and unmanly. Even in her distracted state she could hear how powerless he felt and that irritated her. "What about the army?" he kept saying, "What kind of army we have here? A whole army can't fight against a leader with a bunch of boys?"

Charles called his mother after the broadcast; she had seen it with Robby, his wife Debbie and their children, who Naomi called "the boys". "What would I do without Robby?" Naomi added before she let Charles know that Robby and family had agreed to spend the night with her since she didn't want to leave the house. Charles did not react and said that he would pass by the next morning.

Mrs. B did not call her parents; she wasn't sure where they were or that they would know about the coup. In the last few years, ever since they had got back together (at least for the time being) her mother and father usually travelled during late July and early August to visit family and friends in London. Mrs. B did manage to speak with Aunt Claire, who lived only a short distance away from Naomi. Her aunt sounded worried and anxious but was adamant about not leaving the house. Mrs. B did not insist that Claire should come to them and she felt guilty that she hadn't, but she knew that Claire, whom Charles always found extremely odd, would only add to the stress.

Two days passed. There was a standoff between the Muslimeen, who held hostages inside the parliamentary chamber, and officials on the outside negotiating their release. Two days passed before Larry called to speak with Charles. Mrs. B usually knew to whom Charles was speaking by his tone: the mother tone was tinged with impatience, the office tone, measured or overdone in local dialect depending on whether it was a manager or a worker, but for friends like Larry, it was light, with a lot of chuckles, bordering on adolescent. When she knew it was Larry calling, Mrs. B went to the mirror in the bathroom to see how she looked. She brushed her hair, put on some perfume then sat for a moment on the toilet seat, listening to Charles and Larry talk about which shops were open and protected by army officers. Before she left the bathroom she put on more perfume and took one more glance at her reflection. She had vowed to herself not to ask Charles any questions about the phone call, but the moment he put down the phone she asked who it was.

"Chow, checking to see if we were okay," Charles said, still sounding cheerful.

"And how are they doing?" She tried to sound casual and relaxed.

"Rachel's sister was visiting from California with her kids; they were supposed to fly home tomorrow."

This news upset Mrs. B; Larry hadn't mentioned anything to her about any sister-in-law visiting, but then again he never discussed his life at home. He had a wife, two daughters and a mistress; his life was full of carefully stacked boxes – categorized, separated and stored – much like the warehouses his family owned.

The next few days were even stranger and Mrs. B felt as though she had woken-up in some Fourth World country (Simone's expression). This place was not her home with fires raging in the capital. There was looting everywhere, and the curfews kept them all locked inside, waiting to see how it would all play out.

All this time trapped in the house allowed for moments of reflection, not a common practice for Mrs. B. She tried to think about why she had had the affair with Larry – Larry not Chow; she refused to call him Chow and generally hated the nicknames used by so many grown men on the island. She didn't call Peter "Slims", or Robby "Checkers", so why should Larry be "Chow"? She admitted to herself that she had been attracted to Larry, from the day they first met. In those days Larry and Charles looked alike; they were tall with smooth, dark-brown hair and light golden skin. Like Charles, Larry had some Portuguese blood mixed up with everything, including Chinese, and these mixtures created two wonderful looking specimens. Larry's family had simplified their history by saying they were Portuguese, even though Larry's mother was quite dark, and did not look Portuguese at all, but this they attributed to her claimed Arawak ancestry.

The first time she met Charles, at an Old Year's Night party at the Yacht Club, he introduced her to his good buddy, Larry. Mrs. B barely remembered the evening, having had too much champagne, but she never forgot her girlfriend, Kathy, nudging her to dance with Charles, the Butcher boy. After an awkward dance when they both stepped on each other's toes (for Charles could not lead and barely managed to move) she knew that there was an attraction on both sides. It was after the dance, when Kathy and the other girls conveniently disappeared, that Charles introduced her to Larry who was there with the beauty, Rachel, whom he would marry the same year that she married Charles, each man being the best man at the other's wedding.

★

As Miss Marie Elena Roumain she had made some good attempts at bad behaviour during her sixth-form years at the Convent. Her great aunts had spies everywhere; they lurked in corridors, eavesdropped on students, spoke with teachers and then reported all at tea when her family made their Sunday afternoon visits. The aunts had learnt about Marie Elena's cigarette smoking in the school bathroom, the drinking that took place at a girlfriend's sleepover where the girls spent most of the night guzzling from bottles of gin, vodka and vermouth stolen from the liquor cabinet downstairs, but news of her most embarrassing crime came not from their usual informants but from Sister Mary Margaret herself, vice principal at the convent. It was the case of the forged excuse giving Elena permission to leave the school for a dental appointment, when in fact she had left the school to meet a boy called George, a known delinquent – though from another good family – at an ice cream parlour. Why she'd agreed to meet George had more to do with a truth or dare from the girls in her class rather than any real fondness for the pimply-faced youth. The school itself had dropped the matter; the nuns did not want to embarrass either family; both the Roumains and the Lamberts were generous patrons. In the family, however, the ice-cream parlour incident was neither forgotten nor forgiven; it had embarrassed them – and the old aunts hated to be embarrassed – and they feared that the child was losing her way. But they also had a soft spot for Elena and took into account the cards she had been dealt so early in her life. Her parents had never given her the attention she needed. They sought help and advice from the family priest, Father McCarthy, and spoke to distant relative, Sister Catherine, but neither nun nor priest seemed to have a solution – apart from what the old aunts already knew: she needed her parents. They, at the time, were living in London and felt it best that Elena stay with the family because of this and that and the other. But the old aunts knew that the reason was Simone. Their last hope was Claire.

The next Sunday, immediately after Mass, the driver took Elena to her Aunt Claire's house, the same house she had lived in as a little girl. Although the old Aunts thought Claire a little odd, they still took pride in her demure manner, her work in the church and the way in which she had managed to turn away from a grave mistake committed early in her life. Claire, for her part, had always treated Elena with gentleness and empathy. The old aunts hoped that Claire would be able to steer Elena away from a path that could only lead to shame and embarrassment, from the crushing pain that Claire had experienced from the George Lamberts of her generation.

It was quite some years since Elena had visited Aunt Claire.

Her aunt had been the one to come to the family home when there were large family gatherings. So when Elena walked into the small home she felt like Alice, peeping through the looking glass, for either she had grown extremely tall or everything had become incredibly tiny. Even her aunt seemed smaller. Even under the strained circumstances, Claire could only smile as she saw a lovely sixteen-year-old walk up the short path to the front door. She kissed her niece on both cheeks, offered her a cold drink of grapefruit juice and a slice of warm banana and walnut bread, just out of the oven. Then she took Elena to the small square porch at the side of the house and they sat on two hard white iron chairs with ornate patterns of interlacing vines on the seats. The conversation began gently, and at first Elena was just happy to be in her old home. Very little had changed in the house since she lived there, and very little had changed with her Auntie Claire. She was still very lean, still so soft and kind, but she looked paler and her eyes seemed a little less bright; a simple shift dress fell just above her knees, making her look homely and much older than she probably was.

"Your aunts are very worried about you," Claire said, finally getting enough courage to broach the subject, "only because they are afraid that you will make a terrible mistake."

"I don't know what terrible mistake they expect me to make, Auntie." Elena's reply surprised her aunt. Something about the hard tone brought back memories of her sister, Simone.

"What about the Lambert boy?"

Elena was quick with the retort: "They just don't like the family; they never like anyone I know. Every time I want to go somewhere they ask a million questions, Auntie. It's as though they don't want me to have any friends at all. You know how they are, Auntie, you know." Elena tried not to sound as though she knew too much about what had happened to her aunt, but the question irritated her and she wanted to make her aunt stop.

"I know that they can seem hard at times, but remember they are only trying to protect you."

"Protect me from what, Auntie?" Elena stared at her aunt, sure that she would not want to discuss this. The family had tried to protect Claire, but she hadn't listened. Although she regretted hurting her aunt, Elena soon realised her strategy had worked. Her aunt moved away from the specifics of her niece's behaviour and took refuge in platitudes.

Before the driver returned, Claire, who had known about the visit for at least a week, gave Marie Elena a carefully wrapped gift of one of her favourite books when she was her niece's age; it was *Tess of the D'Urbervilles*.

"It's a book by Thomas Hardy," Claire said quietly. "I liked it…" But she didn't finish the sentence. She wanted to say that maybe they could talk about it one day, but then Claire realised that she was not sure when Marie Elena would visit her again.

Marie Elena never read that book. It was very thick and the print looked extremely small, but she kept it with her and added it to the collection of things that had become important for her to keep. At the gate, before she got into the car, Aunt Claire asked if Elena remembered the family who lived next door, because the eldest boy had got married only to lose his wife to cancer just a year after. Even in repeating the story Claire could feel the tears coming, but it was obvious that Elena was not affected in any way, so she kissed her niece goodbye and stood at the gate until the car disappeared.

Mrs. B remembered telling Larry this story; she thought the Lambert fiasco would amuse him since they still all knew each other. It had, but Larry was more interested in what she had done with George and begged for details, which she was only too happy to invent.

★

There were six days of negotiation between the government and the Muslimeen coup leaders for the hostages' release. Larry had only called that one time; nevertheless Mrs. B managed to convince herself that Larry was trying to send her a message but was finding it too difficult. During the curfew, no one, except perhaps for the hostages themselves, felt as imprisoned as Mrs. B. Instead of trying to make life as pleasant as she could for her family, she behaved like a trapped animal – screaming at Ruthie for the slightest mistake, not letting Charles touch her, rejecting any suggestions to go out and visit family or friends outside of curfew hours.

There were many times when she wanted to drive to Larry's, or call the number without hanging up when Rachel picked up the phone. Mrs. B assumed that Larry was feeling the same way and she let herself imagine he was sending her signs. One day she saw a neighbour's phone bill in her mailbox and she decided it had to have been from Larry; it was his way of telling her to call him, but whenever she built up enough courage, Rachel always seemed to answer.

Although Charles knew that something was wrong with his wife he didn't dare ask. Five years into the marriage and he was afraid that the stroke of good luck that had befallen him would end. He had never seen himself as deserving someone like Marie Elena Roumain and had not given his life much thought until he met and married her. Ambition and success were not things that burned his soul. But he did not want to spoil it all and suddenly wake up one morning to find that it was all part of some cruel joke, that his beautiful wife, daughter, and home had been a hoax. Still, Charles knew that something beyond the events of the coup had his wife in a troubled state.

People found different ways of passing their time during the weeks of the curfew, which continued long after the hostages were released. Night clubs changed their hours, opening from twelve noon to five pm to allow everyone to make it home before the curfew at six; and since it was the long vacation of July and August, students made up a large part of their clientele. Like the rest of her countrymen and women, Mrs. B had taken to drinking a lot more than she used to. Now she had a rum punch before lunch, a couple of glasses of wine during the evening meal and often a little liqueur, usually amaretto, before bed. She spent a lot of time in bed, and only got up when necessary. The television was usually on, magazines were strewn on the floor next to the bed, but she neither read nor really looked at the TV screen. She didn't speak much and even stopped snapping at Ruthie and Charles; she seemed to have difficulty focusing on anything and her state could only be described as trancelike. Charles cared for Ruthie during the curfew. Milly only came for a few hours in the morning and during that time Charles would slip away to the office.

He would have to be home by lunch time, when Milly usually left; when he was stuck at work he would have to call Naomi for help. Mrs. B had never liked having Naomi in her house, but it didn't seem to bother her now and Charles noticed this change in his wife's attitude, but said nothing about it.

★

The Muslimeen surrendered on August 1$^{st}$ after six days of negotiation. Charles and perhaps the rest of the country did not like the way the entire affair had played out. The Muslimeen were taken into custody, tried for treason, but then released because the Court of Appeal upheld the amnesty offered to secure their surrender. "They should have shot them there and then, no need for any damn trial!" Charles became even more vehement in his solution to the problem when the Privy Council later declared the amnesty invalid but the government never re-arrested the Muslimeen. Mrs. B regretted the whole affair. She would tell the story to an older Ruthie, many years later, of driving through the capital weeks after the coup, after the looting, after the fires and simply wanting to cry. The coup had filled her with such sadness, though she would never tell of the other reason; she simply said it was the beginning of the fall and Ruthie took that to mean her country's. "Things would never be the same after this," Mrs. B said, but she knew that the fall was not only her country's but her own.

# CHAPTER FOUR
## MORNINGS

Ruthie emerged from the bedroom in her usual sleepwear of boxer shorts and a loose tank top. It was a Saturday morning so both her parents were home. She kissed them both good morning, poured herself a cup of coffee, added many spoonfuls of sugar and a lot of milk, sat at the bar stool in the kitchen and lingered longer than she normally would. Mrs. B noticed this; she was standing in front of the sink savouring a cup of Blue Mountain coffee. Charles was frying eggs and bacon.

"I went to see Dr. Graham this week." Ruthie paused; her parents said nothing. Ruthie sat there waiting, as though the perfect moment would come for her to deliver the news to her parents. It didn't so she finally said: "Dr. Graham said the tests were positive. He says I am pregnant." Mrs. B thought that she had known this all along. There was silence for what may have been mere seconds but it shook Ruthie and tears started to stream down her face. Charles turned off the stove but did not move towards his daughter. Mrs. B took another sip of her coffee. Ruthie managed to steady herself.

"Is it somebody in Boston?" At home last year, Ruthie had told them of her relationship with someone in Boston, but had omitted the part about the boyfriend being a married professor with two children close in age to Ruthie herself.

"Yes, I think so." Ruthie turned away from her parents to face the other side of the room.

"You *think* so, what the hell do you mean *you think so*?" Charles was shouting now. "I'm talking; you don't turn your damn back on me." He was glaring at his daughter. Mrs. B seldom saw her husband like this, especially when it came to Ruthie. Even with the Boston episode, he had managed to stay calm and steady, at least on the outside. Now he looked as though he could explode and this gave Mrs. B some satisfaction, a let-him-deal-with-it-for-once feeling. But the more questions Charles asked, the more resistant Ruthie became. She had stopped crying now and was looking directly at her father, as though gaining strength from his irrational state. Her seemingly unrepentant manner irritated Charles even more. Who was the father? A student? Older? Younger? American? Black American? (What did that have to do with it, Ruthie interjected.) Did he know about the pregnancy? And what did he plan to do about the situation? Or was it a hit and run? With this last remark, Ruthie walked out of the kitchen, followed by her mother. For a moment at least, allegiances had shifted.

★

Since her return, Ruthie had spent much of the time in her bedroom looking at television, renting movies, talking to American university friends on Facebook or lounging at the hotel pool with a high school friend, Monique Mendoza – a friendship that Mrs. B did not endorse. Monique had been a troublemaker at school, suspended (though not expelled) in her last year for marijuana possession, and then shipped off to a very expensive private school in Barbados, where she continued to cause trouble.

Ruthie had suspected that she was pregnant when the nausea wouldn't go away. Most mornings she could barely face breakfast with her parents. She tried to time her mornings so that she could scrounge around the kitchen after her father had gone to work, her mother had left for the gym, and before Milly came to clean at 8:30 am. In those first few weeks, before Dr. Graham confirmed what the home pregnancy tests had already told her, the thought of an abortion crossed her mind. Then in the doctor's office, when she heard that ridiculously fast heartbeat and saw that black speck, she knew she couldn't; she had to keep the baby.

It took another two weeks before Ruthie told her parents what her friend Monique had known for weeks: the baby was the result of an affair with a married professor from her university. The Professor had received a call soon after Ruthie got the news from

50

Dr. Graham. She finally found him at his office on campus. The Professor was too tactful to ask if she was sure it was his, but then proceeded to tell her how much she had to look forward to in her life, how young she was and how much a baby would change all her plans, ending with "Do you think it's the best time for this, I mean are you going to keep it?" But the baby had gone past the "it" stage for Ruthie.

She cut him short. "Tell me, John, tell me what I have to look forward to. Tell me how great my life is and what a child will take away from me. It's too fucking late for an abortion, John. I'm not going to make life that fucking easy for you…"

John found a way to end the call, claiming that he was making her upset and that it was not good for her health and then Ruthie heard an ever so gentle click. She tried to call him back many times but the phone just kept ringing (he was such a fucking coward) and the thought crossed Ruthie's mind to call John's wife but she didn't, she just couldn't, at least not yet, and so she texted Monique at midnight. Ruthie was barely able to speak but Monique told her that keeping her Professor a secret would just put more stress on her and the baby. The next morning, after a sleepless night, Ruthie kept her promise to Monique; she told her parents about the baby but still felt too much shame to tell them about her Professor.

★

Her mother sat with Ruthie on her unmade bed. She put her hand on Ruthie's back and rubbed it gently; Ruthie was facing the window.

"How many months along are you?"

"About thirteen weeks I think he said." Then she broke down again. Mrs. B had not seen her daughter weep like this, not even in the clinic in Boston.

"We will be fine; it won't seem that way now, but we will be. You mustn't get so upset…" Mrs. B wished she could have cried with her daughter, she wanted to but the tears didn't come and so she just sat there for a few more minutes, then left the room. Charles ate alone on the porch barely tasting the shrivelled bacon and dried eggs.

★

Monique and Ruthie had planned to go to the beach after she told her parents. By the time Monique arrived at 10 am, Charles had already left for the office without saying a word to anyone, though he seldom spent Saturdays there. Mrs. B got ready to go shopping, even though she had done this the day before. As she walked to the car, still in a trancelike state, Ruthie popped her head out of her door and told her that she might go to Maracas. It was the first sunny morning after a month of punishing rain. Mrs. B listed her concerns. The rains had caused landslides along the North Coast Road and the authorities had been asking people to avoid it, but she didn't manage to dissuade her daughter nor did she make any great effort to do so. She touched Ruthie's shoulder but could not bring herself to kiss her. All Mrs. B could think about now was the pregnancy.

Ruthie had to admit that her mother was right, at least about the North Coast Road. It was in the worst shape that she had ever seen it. The red mud from the hills formed a thick layer on the road, and there were broken branches, piles of dead leaves and vines hanging from one side of the road to the other. At one spot, a landslide had blocked half of the road. An uprooted immortelle faced ominously downwards, looking as though it could crash on them with the next downpour. Even more unsettling were the two gigantic boulders balancing at the top of a hill; a mere shower could bring them down onto any passing vehicle.

★

The drive to Maracas, almost every Sunday, used to be something she looked forward to as a child. If they didn't spend the day at the family house down-the-islands on Monos, her mother, father, Granny Naomi, Uncle Robby, Aunt Debbie, cousins and friends would all head to Maracas Beach. Her mother and aunt would have picnic baskets full of snacks and lunch for the adults and children. Ruthie loved her mother's sandwiches and her Granny Naomi's rich chocolate brownies. The men would be in charge of the cooler with gin and tonic for the ladies, beers or scotch for the men, coca cola and juice for the kids. Even with all the food they brought, they would still end up eating warm bake and shark from their favourite vendor. Provided her Uncle Robby didn't forget the cricket bats, the men would play and other families on the beach would just fall into the teams. Without the bats they sometimes used fallen coconut branches. Ruthie and her cousins, Mark and Mathew, would bodysurf the rough Maracas waves. She was a good swimmer and her father always boasted that she was braver than her boy cousins.

★

"They should have closed the road," Ruthie said. Monique had been forced to a crawl to get past all the rocks and red mud.

"They should do a lot of things but they aren't going to do it." Monique kept her eyes focused on the road. Ruthie looked out to the sea; the water was dark, almost black, looking cold, unfriendly. When they got to the lookout, Ruthie asked Monique to stop. This was her first drive to Maracas since she had come home. They got out of the black Prado to admire the view of the tiny islands just off the coast. Strong sunlight re-emerged from behind the clouds, adding a shimmer to the water, and for that small moment Ruthie felt a little better. Monique walked over to the stalls. There were three young women, all in tight blue jeans and bright tank tops, each behind a separate table. They looked related. On the tables were big clear-glass bottles filled with sweet black prunes, bright orange sweet and salt prunes, purple pepper mangoes, and yellow plums, all imported from China. Monique sampled a few stewed prunes she had never seen before. From behind, Ruthie did not look pregnant at all, and had she not said anything, Monique would have thought that she had just gained a little weight around the tummy. They had been friends since high school and their parents, though not close, saw each other at the houses of mutual acquaintances. Even so, for all the time she had known Ruthie, Monique had felt that she was not someone that anyone could get to know very well. There always seemed to be things that Ruthie kept hidden, so when Monique heard about the affair with the Professor, she was not surprised.

"Ready," Ruthie said, after she bought some salted prunes. The winding drive over the hills had made her a little nauseous and the salt supposedly helped. Before they got into the car, Monique took a picture of Ruthie on her cell-phone camera, standing in front of the tall glass bottles filled with multicoloured treats.

"You should record the whole pregnancy. What month is this?"

"Thirteen weeks, just around the third." Ruthie spat out the prune she had tried not to suck while Monique took the photograph. "Okay, I'll hire you as my official photographer. We better get going before my mother has a cow; by now she probably thinks we're over a cliff."

"Call her." Monique offered Ruthie her cell phone.

"No, let her suffer." Ruthie was only half joking.

"That's not nice!" They both laughed.

Monique took a few more photos while they were sitting on the beach; her favourite was the one of Ruthie sitting in the shallow water and rubbing her stomach, giving the baby its first sea bath. By two o'clock they were starving; Ruthie offered to walk over to the food stalls to buy them both a bake and shark.

"My treat," she said, refusing the money from Monique. She took Monique's order carefully. "No garlic sauce, only chadon beni, tambrun sauce, no salad stuff. We Trinis are very particular about what goes on our bake and shark. Not too sure what you Americans like." Monique had been teasing Ruthie since she came back, calling her a damn American.

Ruthie had left her flip-flops in the car, so the hot sand felt like fire under the soles of her feet. The expanse of the bay, the wide beach, the white sand, all took away some of the pain she had felt earlier that morning. There weren't many people on the beach; Saturday was always a quieter day. That was the day that her mother preferred when she was younger. The crowds came on Sunday from every part of the island. Then the beach was like a bazaar, all the vendors out in force, walking up and down: the Indian boys selling bags of peppers, mangoes, limes; Rastas with heavy racks of hanging chains, bracelets and bags made from wooden beads, calabash, and coconut shells; Venezuelans, running from Chavez, selling chains made in China; ice cream vendors with the carts; cotton candy men with racks of pink, blue, and yellow puffs. All the bake and shark huts would be open on Sunday, only half of them on Saturday.

Her parents and cousins usually set up camp close to other friends near the bridge and river, away from the music coming from the bars at the other end of the beach.

Ruthie spotted her favourite vendor, Vera, and ordered two

bakes and shark, a beer for Monique and a sorrel drink for herself. Vera didn't recognize her, but Ruthie remembered her and the daughters who used to help her. One daughter would be kneading the dough for the bakes while the other would be covering the shark cutlets with the flour mixture before her mother dropped them into the pot of hot oil. Ruthie still loved to see the bakes rise and become golden brown balloons as soon as they were dropped into the oil. When the bake and the fried shark cutlets were taken out of the pot, Ruthie could taste it with her eyes. She asked Vera about her daughters, since she was alone today in the shed.

"One in town working now, the other taking classes." Vera answered without taking her eyes off the pot. She looked the same – extremely thick lenses, thin greying hair pulled into a stringy bun and two gold front teeth. She wore a simply cut long dress with a faded floral print and a white apron tied around her waist; she had thin arms and a tiny body, save for a wide waist and paunch. Ruthie remembered how beautiful the daughters were with their long, straight, shiny black hair worn in a long plait that fell just below the waist.

The shed was run down. There was water on the concrete base and the wooden roof was rotting. The paint on the walls, like Vera's red nail polish, was chipped; still she kept the place as neat as she could. All the condiments and dressings were neatly laid out, with plastic covers to keep away the flies and spoons for each of them: garlic sauce, shadon beni, mother-in-law pepper sauce, tamarind sauce, ketchup, lettuce and tomatoes. Ruthie sprinkled on Monique's requests and her own favourites – shadon beni, tamarind sauce, garlic sauce and pepper. Vera wrapped the two bakes in grey sheets of paper, put them in a brown paper bag and gave her two napkins. Ruthie paid and Vera handed her the Heineken and sorrel drink.

"You could manage?" Vera asked.

"Yes, thanks, I'm good." Ruthie smiled and started to make her way back on the hot sand.

There was no reason to feel sorry for Vera; she was managing fine without her daughters, but seeing her alone affected Ruthie. It had to be the baby; she felt like crying for everything these days.

Monique was coming out of the water as she approached. Ruthie had always envied Monique's curves – her tiny waist, her slim torso, a healthy bosom, and rounded derriere, though Monique only ever complained about her looks and was always on one diet or another. Still, whenever they were liming together they always ended up eating something delicious and fattening: doubles, roti and bake and shark. After she left for university, Ruthie had not kept in touch with the few friends she had made at high school, but there was something different about Monique. She admired Monique's honesty, her candidness about herself and others. Her opinions were seldom remarkable, her arguments lacked subtlety but her advice was reliable in a precise, practical way.

"So what's the story with your professor?" Monique said, putting on a short floral sarong over her red bikini bottom. "Is he coming here?"

"Are you mad? Why would he come here?" Ruthie handed over Monique's beer and her bake and shark.

"Thanks. This smells so good. Where did you go, Vera?"

Ruthie nodded and Monique took another big bite.

"He wouldn't want to see his own child?"

Ruthie welcomed Monique's direct approach. At home, her parents would ask about the baby's father even if they wanted to; they would wait for Ruthie to tell them. That was how it was in her family; unpleasant subjects were always avoided or dealt with in a distant manner, as though they were happening to someone else.

"He won't do anything; I am sure he won't come here. I mean he won't even act as though he has a child. Listen, trust me, he's definitely not coming."

"Did he actually say that you should have a fucking abortion?"

"He said I had so much to look forward to… which translates as abortion."

"Well I would have missed that one for sure."

They both laughed and for the rest of the afternoon they spoke about silly things or nothing at all. Monique flipped through copies of *Self*, *Shape* and *Elle* and Ruthie read a story from Alice Munro's recent book, *Too Much Happiness*. Every once in a while, when it was just too hot, Monique went into the sea for a dip and tried to persuade Ruthie to join her; eventually Ruthie did and they had a great time bobbing over the waves and chatting.

★

Mrs. B could not see a way out. Ruthie occupied her thoughts from the moment she opened her eyes to the last thought at night. On the treadmill at the gym, kneeling in church, handing out lunches at the soup kitchen, her thoughts always returned to Ruthie. Charles and she spoke of little else; they had little else to speak about. She sought solace in a few trusted friends who recommended different remedies but absolutely nothing – not yoga, not Oprah, not *The Power of Now*, not even a case of Pinot grigio – helped her present state of mind. Mrs. B used to feel that she had paid her dues as a child, and now was owed a better life. This had shaken her faith; it had been a mistake to imagine that she could buy insurance from the universe, or make a pact with God. Adding to her stress was Ruthie's renewed friendship with Monique, who was rumoured to be having an affair with a married man, a very rich, powerful Syrian. She tried to bring up the subject with Charles.

They were in the living room; Charles was reading a front-page story involving torture and sodomy before the victim, a ten year old boy, was strangled.

"What do you think of that Mendoza girl?" Mrs. B tried her best to sound neutral.

"She seems okay. It's good for Ruthie to have someone here, at home." Charles read on. The second paragraph went on to say that the boy's father was an alleged drug dealer in the south of the island; the journalist attributed the killing as a payback for some deal gone sour.

"You know she is having an affair with that awful Nadir man."

"The son?"

"No, the father."

"Who told you that?" Charles put down the paper; he knew the Nadir family well. The sons had recently acquired two beautiful fishing boats in Miami and spent a lot of money at "Go Fish", the business that Robby managed.

"I don't want Ruthie with someone who is with a man like that.

I mean Ruthie didn't spend so much time with her in high school. Why is she doing all these things with her now?"

Charles could see that his wife was upset, close to tears, so he didn't say that Ruthie, pregnant and unwed, was not exactly a symbol of perfection, and perhaps that was why she felt so comfortable with Monique, but said, "We can't expect her to be alone now, I mean, to have no friends, especially during this time; it's hard to come back and fall right back in. Her friends are still away…"

"Alone? She isn't *alone*, Charles. She has us, and other friends besides that Mendoza girl; she has her cousins. I don't understand Ruthie's choices any more. It's just too much, this, everything, the entire situation, too much." She got up from the sofa and went upstairs; Charles did not follow her.

There was more on his mind today than Ruthie's condition, and this was rare because since she had given them the news, Charles's thoughts had kept returning to the pregnancy and he knew it was the same for his wife. He was thinking about the ten year old boy who had paid a price that his killers would never pay. Recently, a friend, another businessman, had been shot and robbed as he left the bank on Friday afternoon with cash to pay his workmen. A Friday afternoon on one of the busiest streets in Port-of-Spain and no one could give a description of the bandits. One person saw a black Nissan sedan and two black men. Another saw two Indians and a dougla woman in a blue Toyota. Charles couldn't blame anyone these days for not speaking up; witnesses had been killed on the steps of the courthouse. He wanted to talk to Chow and find out about the friend who was still in hospital, but as he picked up the phone he heard his wife's voice on the line, probably complaining about him to one of her friends. Charles shrugged and put down the phone.

# CHAPTER FIVE
## NEWS

If life inside the Butcher household was not going as planned, what was happening outside was worse. No one was quite sure when it started, no one could put a date on it, no one could say, *Look, that was exactly the moment when we left one world and entered another*, but now it was obvious to almost everyone in the country, except to the President himself (sometimes called the Emperor, as in the Emperor's New Clothes, or Ali Baba, as in Ali Baba and the forty thieves) that he had turned the corner, lost his marbles, gone clear, completely clear. But this was never said in public. The President had his spies in the parliament, in the senate, at TV stations, radio stations, any and everywhere. They tapped phones, tracked emails, even installed cameras in bathrooms. The fear of discovery and its often fatal consequence kept much of the information at an almost inaudible level. Mothers, fathers, grandmothers, grandfathers, aunts and uncles lost sleep at night wondering how much worse things could get for their children, grandchildren, nephews and nieces. When a brave, reckless, or simply foolish citizen wrote a letter to the editor exposing some corrupt act, it was never published. No one blamed the newspapers for the silence, especially since a female journalist and big-time Sunday editor were both shot in the head at point blank range as they stepped onto the pavement at ten o'clock one night, leaving a popular rum shop in St. James. The killers didn't even wear masks. They simply walked up to them and shot. Many saw, but the killers knew that no one would dare identify them in any police lineup; "doh fucking say nothing" were their last words as they got into the waiting vehicle. So when the police arrived half an hour later, although the Police Station was only minutes away, nobody said fucking nothing. Nobody from the sizeable Saturday night crowd saw the killers' faces, nobody could say what they wore, nobody could describe the getaway car.

The same people, who a week earlier had said in private that the editor was so brave, now muttered that he was foolhardy, crazy and that his drinking had led him to this mad decision. The editor and his journalist had gone into very unsafe territory, accusing the President and his band of forty thieves of corruption. And it was not as though the editor had chosen one of the more horrific crimes. He had exposed what he thought might be considered a "small" offence, and pointing only indirectly to the President and members of his cabal; it concerned a four billion dollar housing project that had been in the works for the last eight years. There was much more the editor could have said – how many pretty young girls had been packed like sardines into containers with cocaine being shipped to Russia via Panama and Philadelphia; how many eyewitnesses had been shot in the witness protection programme (many people did not even know it existed); how many powerful businessmen were generals in the gang wars, giving orders to lieutenants who then passed on the instructions to their army of sixteen-year-old foot soldiers. There was so much more he could have said, so much more. But many citizens, including those in the Butcher circles, believed that though the country was in a bad way, no doubt about it, things could be worse. What about Somalia, Angola, what about the Taliban, or Afghanistan or even just across the road in Venezuela? At least they didn't have a Chavez or a Castro telling them what to do. They didn't have anyone ordering them to give up their land or their island homes. Even in America there were twice as many murders, kidnappings, rapes, stabbings, shootings, and car-jackings; and think about it, much of what was happening was gang related – an eye for an eye and those who lived by the sword and so on, so let them kill each other.

Two days after the killings, there was a rumour on the Internet that the editor, recently estranged from his second wife, was having an affair with the pretty journalist. There was also a picture taken from the journalist's Facebook page of her in a skimpy bathing suit at Maracas. The story claimed the journalist was once a "hostess" working in a seedy night club in St. Joseph before she started at the paper. The killing was a crime of passion ordered by a jealous boyfriend who was an ex-customer at the club. Soon the rumour made its way into a rival daily newspaper in an article that supported the Internet story. The shooting was definitely the result of a love affair gone sour, but the perpetrators and boyfriend were still at large, so naturally investigations were continuing.

★

Once a month, Mrs. B had lunch with her close friends. When the hostess took Mrs. B across to their table, Kathy was already there. It was one of their favourite places to lunch, with a view of the sea and the boats in the harbour. The large dining room was elegantly simple: teak tables and chairs, pinewood floors, white tablecloths, with miniature red anthuriums in small clay pots at the centre of the table. The large wooden windows opened to frame the extended seascape. As she approached, Kathy quickly put an end to her cell-phone conversation, stood up and kissed her.

"Kathy, you're so good, always on time. Sorry to be a little late. You look great." Mrs. B was pleased to notice that her friend, who had been on a three-week Mediterranean cruise, had gained a few pounds. "How was the cruise?"

"Great, but I ate like a damn pig. Too much food on those damn things. All you do is eat and then line up to eat again." Kathy, who had always struggled with her weight, believed in tight clothing – one size larger, Mrs. B concluded, and her black trousers and white sequined tank would have looked more elegant. Still, Mrs. B admired Kathy's beautiful necklace and diamond pendant, an early Christmas gift from her husband, bought at a stop in Venice. But Kathy's looking plump put Mrs. B in a better frame of mind since she was not feeling particularly attractive herself.

"No, you really look great, Kath," Mrs. B said again, looking towards one of the waitresses at the bar.

"Well I feel like a fat cow. You on the other hand look so trim. Still at the gym?"

"Not much, but life can be a great diet." Mrs. B laughed but Kathy saw she wasn't joking. Ruthie's return had taken its toll; her friend looked thin rather than trim, her face drawn and strained.

"How's Ruthie doing? Found a job yet?" Mrs. B knew that the

question Kathy really wanted to ask was about Ruthie's pregnancy and the identity of the baby's father.

"She's fine, no job yet. Not sure if it makes sense anyway, especially now, but she's doing fine."

"So, is she going to stay here, or go back to Boston?" Kathy was looking closely for her friend's reaction, hoping for some clue to see if the father was, as everyone suspected, a Bostonian. Mrs. B had not told Kathy all the details. Kathy's nickname was CNN; her friends only told her what they wanted the world to know.

"Why would she go back to Boston?" Mrs. B replied calmly. "We have great doctors here who can handle any problem." Kathy looked cornered and they both took a sip of the slightly chilled house white they had ordered. As though on cue, Jackie, the third member of their lunch party entered the restaurant looking like some Hollywood starlet with her Chanel shades, white jeans and white, Mexican-inspired tunic with an embroidered neckline of tiny black wooden beads. Jackie was tall, very slim, fair-skinned, with short straight dark brown hair that fell just above her shoulders. She looked a lot like Mrs. B, and strangers had often thought that they were sisters, but Mrs. B was shorter and her eyes were darker and smaller. Jackie had very fine features, with the exception of her mouth – which seemed to be in a perpetual pout. Kathy said it gave her an Angelina look. Because of her very fair, almost milky skin, everyone said that Jackie looked like her father who was English, with the same pout for a mouth. In truth, Jackie looked more like her mother, who was very dark, but with the same fine features.

Kathy had once said to Mrs. B that Jackie had really done well for herself, "considering everything". Mrs. B knew what Kathy meant and that for all their years of friendship, Kathy's family background would never completely allow her to see Jackie as an equal. Jackie's mother, an Indian from Caroni, had worked as a servant in Jackie's father's house. An oil company man, Jackie's father earned US dollars and lived the lifestyle that went with it.

Kathy knew the whole story, how the affair had forced the first Mrs. Gilmour to return to England with Jackie's two half-brothers; how Miss Sheila, as she was known in the Gilmour household, moved into the house to eventually become Mrs.

Gilmour number two. It was the early sixties, 1962 in fact, when Margaret Gilmour left the island, the same year that Jackie Gilmour was born.

If Jackie was still lovely in her forties, in her early twenties she had been embarrassingly beautiful; people stared at her as if bewitched and this led to uncomfortable feelings all round. But Jackie was not vain. In fact she lived with a voice that told her every morning how lacking she was in every aspect of her life.

At lunch, the three friends, who had known each other in high school, usually began by comparing notes on their children's lives. Once, Mrs. B had looked forward to these chats but now she had very little to say. Jackie's daughters, who had not started off as brilliantly as Ruthie, were now on their way to careers in law and dentistry. Kathy had three children – two girls and a boy; one of the girls was already married and ran a kindergarten school; the second was soon to be married and both daughters had married boys from established families in the north. She didn't, though, say much about her fourteen-year-old son who had been suspended twice in the last term from his expensive private school. She blamed the school for constantly targeting him but Jackie and Mrs. B had heard that Brandon had been involved in several fights and had threatened a female teacher. There was a rumour going around that he had brought a knife to school. Mrs. B did not wish this pain on Kathy, but Brandon's behaviour gave her some consolation.

With Christmas fast approaching, they spoke about shopping in Miami to buy gifts and things for their homes. This year Jackie's younger daughter was thinking of sharing a container with another newlywed couple so she could ship furniture and appliances for her new house. They barely discussed the journalist and editor story, though Kathy said that she had heard that the editor's estranged wife was having an affair with some Negro boy she had met on the beach in Tobago.

"You heard anything about that thing with that Mendoza girl?" Kathy asked, taking a small bite from her salmon.

"Which one of the girls? Monique?" Jackie asked.

Kathy nodded. "Monique. Yes, Monique because Maria lives in Barbados now. Monique always gave them a hard time, always in trouble. But I heard from a very reliable source that Missy is with someone we know, a married man, same age as Monique's father. So, I'll give you three guesses, no two, one each."

Kathy was enjoying this, she loved giving them the latest gossip, and nine out of ten times she was right. She took a sip of her wine and stared at them both. Mrs. B thought Kathy was going to confirm what she had heard about Monique and the Nadir man, but neither she nor Jackie would hazard a guess and Kathy could not wait.

"Chow? You mean Chow who is in church every Saturday for six o'clock Mass, who never forgets to open the door for his beloved Rachel?" Now it was Jackie's turn to enjoy the gossip; she thought Rachel extremely snobbish, feeling that she had never truly accepted her as part of the group.

"The very same, and they say Rachel knows but is just trying to brush it off." Kathy and Jackie laughed, then took a sip of their drinks as though toasting Rachel's demise. They were so amused that they only belatedly noticed that Mrs. B was silent.

"Please don't tell me you're sorry for that ice queen," Kathy said. "You were the one who called her a *chienne*."

"No, it's just that Monique has been spending time with Ruthie, and I heard through the grapevine, someone at the hairdressers, that she was having an affair with the Nadir man."

"I heard that too, but it's not true. I have a good source. That little prostitute is with Chow."

"I wouldn't put it past Chow, always making a pass at somebody, not so, Jackie?" Kathy laughed.

Mrs. B's head was starting to spin. She did not want to ask Jackie whether Chow had made a pass at her (he probably had), and she really didn't want to hear any more about Monique.

"Everyone knows about Chow's escapades," Jackie said. "Rachel is always the last to know, poor thing, but she's such a bitch, always smiling and pleasant, but stabbing you in the back every chance she gets."

Jackie had never forgiven the reaction of Rachel and her friends when she had described her wedding day. It was at a party at Chow's house on Monos, soon after Jackie had moved north with her husband, who was very friendly with Chow. Jackie, trying to impress her new friends, told them about her recent wedding, describing a chocolate fountain that was in the shape of a cow, the five hundred guests, and the limbo and Indian dancers. They had all been politely smirking at the bizarre details, but when Rachel asked whether it was a show or a wedding, they all burst out laughing.

While Jackie and Kathy were crucifying Rachel, Mrs. B was doing some arithmetic. As she counted the years, taking away 1990 from 2009, she knew that too much time had passed for any feelings to be still there, especially from such a brief affair. The problem was she had never really stopped seeing Larry. They both had to continue as though nothing had happened. Larry did this well; no one could tell at the dinner parties or the limes on Monos. The two families remained close; the secret was safe.

"Lena, hello. Anyone in there?" Kathy called over the waitress to order dessert: cappuccinos and amaretto cheese cake times three. Kathy's diet, after three glasses of wine, was out of the window.

For the rest of the afternoon, Kathy and Jackie continued to slaughter Rachel, put Chow in front of a firing squad, and predict a life of prostitution for Monique. Lunch ended at about three thirty when, slightly tipsy, they kissed and hugged in the restaurant car park, promising to get together more often in the new year.

"Stay tuned," Kathy said, before she drove off in her new Audi, a birthday gift from her husband.

"I'll call you soon," Mrs. B managed to say with a smile, but on the way home the tears came.

★

The very next day, Mrs. B did something she had been wanting to do but had been avoiding for a long time. She called Larry. It was Wednesday, so she called him at work. His secretary passed on the call from Mrs. Elena Butcher.

"Lena, what's up?" She felt nervous at the sound of his voice; he always sounded so youthful, not the forty-eight year old businessman often seen sipping cocktails with ministers and the President in the "Special Occasions" section of the newspapers.

"I was just calling to see how you were doing," she said, trying hard not to sound the way she really felt.

"I'm great. How 'bout you? I saw Charlie boy yesterday."

"Really, where?"

"Ordering doubles in front of the grocery." Larry sounded very relaxed.

"Listen, I don't want to waste your time. I know how busy it is at work."

Larry said he was never too busy to talk to her.

"I called because I wanted to talk to you about something I heard." She left it hanging, waiting for him to take the bait.

"Yeah, what's that?"

"It's about the Mendoza girl, Monique."

"Yeah, what did you hear?"

"I just thought you should know…" Mrs. B was beginning to lose courage. She was not good at this; she lacked Kathy's bravado.

"Know what? Come on, enough games, Lena. What is it?" Larry tried to sound calm but she could tell he was a little irritated, or nervous.

"It's about you and Monique."

"*Me* and Monique?" He was definitely sounding angry now and was not trying to hide it.

"I heard that there was something going on between…"

Larry cut her off immediately. "This is what you call to tell me, Lena? That I am having something with my daughter's friend? Are you going mad? Who told you this shit? No, wait, let me guess. It must be Jackie. That bored bitch has not a damn thing to do but try to…"

"Why are you calling Jackie a bitch? You don't even know if she said it."

"Okay, so tell me. Was it Jackie or not?" His tone was bullying, "And I'm sure you stood up for me, right?"

"Sure I did, Larry, because you have such a great track record with these things."

Larry tried to calm down again. He didn't like to lose his cool; to relinquish any control to the other person – wife, ex-lover, child, business partner or minister – was a sign of weakness.

"You know what, Lena? Let's just drop it. Listen to me well; there is nothing going on. Even the idea of it is just sick, sickening and that's all I can tell you. It's really up to you to decide who and what you believe. Listen I have to go. We'll catch up soon."

She said goodbye and deeply regretted the call.

★

The next day Monique came to visit Ruthie, who had been having a very bad day; she was nauseous again, and had vomited a few times. The doctor had said the nausea would probably stop after the first trimester, but Ruthie, who was now almost at the end of her second, was still nauseous. She felt too sick to eat but was hungry. She hated herself, her body; at times she even hated the baby, but would never admit this to anyone.

Mrs. B had heard the call from the guards at the gate, informing them of Monique's arrival. From the side porch where she was checking on a newly potted mint plant, she heard Ruthie open the door. A moment later she heard Monique's sing song voice and then heard Ruthie laugh for the first time in what felt like months. They went to the kitchen and Mrs. B could smell curry. In spite of the nausea, curry was what Ruthie craved.

"Do you think that curry is the best thing now, sweetie?" Mrs. B asked, trying her best not to sound too intrusive.

"Hi Auntie, I didn't know you were here," Monique said. "I'm sorry. I brought the roti for Ruthie."

"Hi, Monique," Mrs. B replied. "Thanks. That was nice of you, and if the mummy-to-be wants a roti, then roti it is."

"That's what I feel like eating, Mum," Ruthie said, inviting Monique onto the patio at the back of the house. Expressions like "mummy-to-be" made her want to scream, especially since it made the pregnancy sound planned. At this point Ruthie had absolutely no desire to be a mummy.

Mrs. B wondered if Monique had told Ruthie about Larry. She made another rare attempt to examine her feelings; the thought of this girl with Larry made her angry, jealous, envious, unhappy, foolish – these were unsubtle reactions she could understand – but then there was a titillating one that brought back the old days with Larry, when they met in secret. She felt as though she was competing with a sexy, twenty-something and, for some inexplicable reason, it made her feel attractive, young, not passé, not old. Because for so long Mrs. B had been filled with cloudy feelings, they had taken over slowly, insidiously. She had been living an unexamined life, without reflection, only reactions. She could only say that she felt lost, even before Ruthie's return, even before that awful episode in Boston. She had achieved so little in her life and there seemed to be so little to look forward to, even though Charles had never accused her of being a bad wife, nor had Ruthie ever said that she was a bad mother. But then, indulging in reflection led to self-pity, and her family did not believe in this, it was frowned upon, considered weak, so she put her cloudy mood down to the call to Larry and vowed never to call him again about the Monique story.

★

"Too much pepper?" Ruthie had barely touched her chicken roti.

"No, sorry, but I just can't seem to get it down."

"Why are you sorry? I understand. No, not true. I don't have a clue but I truly sympathize." And Monique's wide friendly smile made Ruthie smile too.

"It must be so frigging hard now. It *has* to be hard now."

"Yeah and the more I read about labour, the more I think I'm going to ask for the drugs – to hell with natural, give me the frigging drugs now." Ruthie tried to laugh, but it sounded strained.

"I'll be there if you want, I mean in the room or whatever." Monique touched Ruthie's arms gently; no one had actually held her or touched her in that way for months; it was not the Butcher family way. Ruthie felt tears coming and she didn't want to cry in front of her friend, or on the back porch in view of some nosy neighbour, and she didn't want her mother to see, but her watery eyes gave her away.

"It'll be fine, Ruthie, everything will work out fine. It will, it has to."

Mrs. B, looking on from inside the kitchen, was trying to casually *maco* the conversation; she did not want to go outside to face Monique who was able to comfort her daughter in a way she knew she couldn't. In the last month, she had consciously tried to keep her distance – unless Ruthie asked her to perform a specific task. Mrs. B had gone to all the visits to the doctor's, booked the nursing home, offered to go to Lamaze classes with her, but Ruthie did not want to go. Already, Mrs. B had packed the suitcase with the list from the nursing home. She had done what

68

she thought a mother of a pregnant daughter was supposed to do. Ruthie had been polite about it all, had thanked her mother several times for everything, but not once had she confided in her mother, talked about how she felt about having a baby without the father around, or how she felt about being at home in this state. Ruthie revealed none of these things to her mother and Mrs. B did not insist. Not even on the night that she went into Ruthie's room after she heard her speaking angrily to someone on the phone, crying through her anger, unable to control the level of the voice. When Mrs. B had opened the door, Ruthie turned to her and asked for "a little privacy". Mrs. B could not sleep for the rest of that night. Her daughter's face haunted her; she looked exhausted, haggard, distraught. When Mrs. B woke Charles to tell him that she thought Ruthie was talking to the father, Charles grunted something inaudible, turned away from his wife and went back to sleep.

★

Monique spent the whole day with Ruthie. They chatted on the back porch, then went to the video club at the mall and borrowed a few movies. Ruthie craved cheesy popcorn so they popped a few bags. Mrs. B did notice that once or twice Monique took cell phone calls away from Ruthie's earshot. Mrs. B could only wonder if it was Larry. When Charles came back from the office that afternoon he found his daughter happily enjoying a comedy with Monique. He found his wife lying stiffly in bed reading a book and in an extremely sour mood. It was as though the two women had traded places for the day.

# CHAPTER SIX
## FINE WINE

For the first time in years Mrs. B did not want to buy a costume to play mas. In fact she dreaded the thought of the parade of bands on Carnival Monday and Tuesday. All of her friends played in the same Carnival band, often in the same section, so it would be almost impossible to avoid seeing Larry for the two days when the band would take the group of three thousand revellers through the streets of Port of Spain to the Savannah. But deciding not play was not a simple thing. Mrs. B had played mas since she was seventeen in the same band with people she had known all her life. Mrs. B and Charles, Jackie and Sparky, Kathy and Joey shared a cart. They had always hired the same group of muscled men to push their drinks in the cart through town on Monday and Tuesday; the hired men served them their drinks and provided security. Not playing was not an individual decision. Mrs. B and her friends were like a band inside a band; she would have to explain why she didn't want to play and she could never tell the truth, that for the first time in many years the idea of seeing Larry and Rachel together was too painful.

It was not hard for Mrs. B to imagine the two Carnival days; the scene was predictable down to a drunken fight that usually took place on Tuesday at around six in the evening. The only thing that changed from year to year was the music and the fact that their bodies had grown older, losing the glow of the young skin that the twenty-somethings in the band didn't even care about. Other than that, everything else was the same: same costume, different colour, same place at the back of the band where there was always more room to move around. Mrs. B and her small tribe seldom strayed from the moving cart of drinks; they would be chipping, jumping, or wining alongside one of the long flatbed music trucks where the DJs would be blasting the soca of the season. Still, for all the sameness, there were moments at Carnival that Mrs. B loved, like Carnival Monday morning, usually around ten o'clock, walking in her costume towards the band's mas camp, where thousands of revellers would gather to move through the streets of Port of Spain. They waited in the hot sun, drinking, laughing, hugging, filling the street with bikinis, beads, feathers and waves of colour: pink, blue, white, red, aquamarine, turquoise, green, gold and silver. She loved it, too, when the music started and everything began to move, masqueraders, revellers, music trucks, drink carts, security, band leaders and those who just followed the band along the pavements, giving the costumed revellers the road.

Mrs. B liked the overlap, the crossover from J'ouvert to Monday Mas, from dirty mas to pretty mas, one part of the festival ending with another about to begin, when the pretty Monday morning masqueraders tried their best to avoid being soiled as their paths crossed with the J'ouvert early morning revellers who were always stale drunk, tired, happy with bodies covered in mud or cocoa or blue-devil paint. She had never played J'ouvert followed by Monday Mas. Charles, Sparky and Joey had done this once and they barely survived; only the truly brave could do this. According to Sparky, that kind of partying took months of training.

At Carnival time, Mrs. B and Larry greeted each other the same way, simply as good old friends who could share a joke, a little gossip. As the day went on and everyone drank more scotch, beers, vodka, or shots of tequila, Larry would hold onto her waist from behind and no one thought anything of it, even though Larry's touch sent a shiver through Mrs. B's spine, but that was for Mrs. B to know and no one else. Holding on to someone else's wife in the band was allowed, even encouraged by the spouse, so he or she would have permission to do the same; but despite this bourgeois lusting, middle-class groping and upper class grinding, the band-members followed certain codes of behaviour. In the presence of a husband or wife, the wine with a non significant other could be enjoyed in a fairly controlled manner. It could cause amusement but not discomfort and it should never embarrass. Wives should not wine with or on the strapping black security guards before Tuesday afternoon or late Tuesday evening (and then only briefly) when the festivities were coming to an end and the rules were a little more relaxed. Away from the husband's or wife's radar, more freedom with the wining partner was allowed and the length of contact could be extended. But unless an undercover couple was seen leaving the band together in the morning and only returning after many hours of absence, all was generally forgiven. As Mrs. B's father once said, Bacchus was on call and Jesus had a holiday until Ash Wednesday.

Mrs. B was not one of those wives who used Carnival as a time to escape from Charles; her faithful Charles was usually at her side and he seldom made her uncomfortable. Her only worry was that he had a tendency to drink too much and she often had to drive them home at the end of the day. Once or twice she had to ask one of his friends (usually Sparky or Joey, never Chow) to help her get Charles to the car. Still, apart from these few occasions and one or two squabbles when alcohol had led Mrs. B to some irrational conclusions about Charles and a breast-implanted Dutch tourist, Carnival was generally a time that both the Butchers looked forward to and enjoyed.

But now the thought of Carnival Monday and Tuesday in the band was stressful; Larry, unlike Charles, was one of those men who would wander off for a couple of hours and return to their cart for a drink, though when he did return to his particular spot, he would quickly reclaim possession of Rachel, considered one of the most beautiful ladies of a certain age in the band. Rachel had been a dancer and was now a part-time Pilates instructor, so she was still very slim and very toned. Her thick, dirty-blond hair fell to the small of her back. Her skin looked forever tanned (her father, although fair in complexion, had come from a mixed background) and her mother's Irish heritage had given Rachel a pair of piercing blue eyes. In her skimpy bikini costume, with beads dangling, she was a threat to the self-esteem of any woman who dared to stand or wine next to her. Larry beamed with pride when he held on to Rachel's small waist; he knew the effect she had on both males and females. The thought of Larry in the band with Rachel was bad enough, but the idea of him stealing away to have some quick, slutty hook-up with Monique made Mrs. B nauseous, dizzy and unhinged.

So Mrs. B could not tell Charles the real reason for not wanting to play mas this year, even though they had already paid down on two costumes. She thought of excuses she could use. There was the crime situation, but Charles, and everyone else was well aware that the country was usually at its safest on Carnival Monday and Tuesday; bandits organized most of their criminal activities earlier in the season; the end was mainly left for partying. Furthermore, government ministers usually played in the pretty bands with their bodyguards and the President brought out the army and police to protect the tourists. Once in a while there was a murder, and sometimes there were stabbings, usually during J'ouvert (last year one man was shot in the groin for wining on someone else's girlfriend), but this was mild compared to the crimes committed during the rest of the year. Mrs. B realized that she had to draw Charles' attention to what mattered most in his life – Ruthie. Who would stay with Ruthie? What if she went into labour?

"This is not a good time to leave her alone." Mrs. B was making a spinach and mushroom quiche for lunch while Charles was flipping through the newspaper. Ever since his wife had mentioned the Carnival issue, he had begun to feel uneasy, not sure what route she was about to take or what he should say to avoid any more tension.

"Maybe she could stay with a friend. What about Monique? Is she playing?" Charles was not thinking when he made this suggestion, and it did exactly what he had been trying to avoid – sent his wife over the tipping point.

"Monique? Of all people *that* is who you think should take care of Ruthie? You know I don't trust that girl. Why did you think of her?" She stopped preparing lunch and looked at Charles, who continued to stare at a classified ads.

"Why did you think of *her?*" Mrs. B asked again. "What is this constant desire to paint this girl in the most angelic light when we all know that she has so many issues? You know I don't like her spending all this time with Ruthie."

Charles was not sure why Monique so enraged his wife. He

put it down to jealously; she was competing with Monique for Ruthie's attention and trust. Charles had never believed the rumour of the affair with Nadir.

"Why don't you answer me, Charles? Our daughter is about to have her first baby, your first grandchild and you are suggesting that we leave her in the hands of that girl?"

Charles ventured a response: "I only said Monique because Ruthie seems very comfortable..." But his wife cut him off.

"How do you know who she's comfortable with? When have you been around to even notice? You're never here. In fact you never seem to be around when there's a crisis, any crisis. I can always count on you to disappear like a frigging coward – always running away..."

But rather than weaken him, as these attacks usually did, they emboldened him; these were old themes that she pulled out from the bag of complaints whenever she wanted to wound him. Twenty-odd years was more than enough time to learn the rules of engagement. Ever since Ruthie had been hospitalized in Boston and he had not accompanied her, his wife had felt that she had this grenade (or a stock pile of them) that she could lob into any fight at any time. He would usually run for cover or comply. This time, for some reason, he spoke up.

"I don't see anything wrong with Monique; she's been a good friend to Ruthie. She talks to her more than us. *You* have a problem with Monique. Ruthie and I don't." Charles had raised his voice enough for his wife to wonder if the neighbours could hear; in the valley she could scream at Charles without once thinking about the neighbours.

"*I* have a problem with Monique? What problem could *I* possibly have with that girl? She is the one who throws herself at every married man that comes her way... but if I said who is the latest... Anyway, I'm not going to tell you what I heard about that girl. I promised Kathy, but even you, Charles, would be shocked." Mrs. B could feel everything inside welling up. He had cornered her, but she wasn't quite ready to tell Charles what Kathy had told her about Larry.

"Everyone knows that Kathy always has information on somebody; you've said so yourself, so..."

She didn't let him finish. "Right, Charles, you win. I'll say it. That Monique you so want to defend, for whatever reason, is having an affair with a married man who you know."

"Yes, Nadir, you said that before…"

"No, Charles, not Nadir. Someone else, someone you know – a good friend in fact." She wished she could have retrieved those words, pulled them right back and placed them under lock and key.

"Really? Who is it? Whose reputation is Kathy destroying now?"

Mrs. B could not bring herself to say that it was Chow. "If you want Ruthie to spend time with someone who has such a terrible reputation, that's fine, but I have a major problem with that, Charles."

"You don't want to say who this *friend* is?" Charles's tone troubled Mrs. B. He was not shouting but she sensed a deep anger.

Mrs. B could only retreat. She left the kitchen and the quiche in an uncovered bowl exposed to any passing fly, and when she got to the top of the stairs she slammed the bedroom door. For effect, Charles concluded.

# CHAPTER SEVEN
## TROPHIES

After his wife stormed off, Charles had to get out of the house, which felt even smaller than it did the first day they moved in. Luckily the keys to the SUV were on the counter next to the phone so he didn't have to go into their bedroom. He had his home clothes on, old khaki shorts and a faded blue polo shirt that he sometimes wore to cricket practice, but he didn't care.

He would spend the rest of that Saturday at the office. He would buy a shrimp roti and a Coke from Mary's, the roti shop next to his office building, and eat his lunch at his desk. There was some paperwork to be done, but mostly Charles just sat and stared at the objects around the room. On the shelf above some of the filing cabinets were old trophies that his father had won in fishing competitions throughout the Caribbean, with the two his father treasured most – from a tournament in Miami – at the front of the collection. Charles and Robby had accompanied their father on some of these competitions, particularly the ones in Tobago. One trophy, a favourite of his and his father's, was in the form of a marlin hanging upside down as though it was about to be weighed. There was a photograph of the two boys standing on either side of their father holding this trophy. Robby looked more like their father, not only because they shared the same golden-brown tan, the long lean face, the thick dark brown hair and the aquiline nose (Charles looked more like his mother), but his father and Robby also shared a smile that captured the happiness of the moment, while Charles looked nervous, even anxious.

Next to his father's awards were Ruthie's. She had won trophies throughout primary school and high school for every-thing from scripture to art, for languages, always literature and history and even, once, for chemistry. On another shelf there were photographs of his wife and daughter taken on vacations all over the world. Not a single trophy belonged to Charles, nor was he in any of the photographs save the one with Robby and their father.

Two years before the attempted coup in 1990, his father had died of a heart attack while working on the engine of his boat, *Naomi*. Every boat had been named after his wife. "Beauty of a wife, beauty of a boat," his father would say, even though in the last few years he seemed to be spending more time with "the mistress" (his boat) rather than "the Missus" (his wife). Although they had spent many weekends with their father down-the-islands on *Naomi*, fishing for hours on end, Charles and Robby decided to sell their father's boat soon after his death. They didn't think they would be using it as much without their father around to organize the fishing excursions. They also had their own boats, though they were not as beautiful as *Naomi*. After their father died, the brothers started to lease the family home on Monos, but they always had it for two weeks in August and two weeks at Easter. The Easter weeks were reserved for their mother who loved waking up close to the water on Palm Sunday and attending Mass at the small chapel built at the back of a friend's house on the island of Gasparee. Easter had always been an important time for the family. When they were young, Naomi loved the ritual of waking the boys up early (she included her husband in the collective "boys"), feeding them with buljol, coconut bake, smoked herring and fresh grapefruit juice, and ensuring that every man jack was in their Sunday best before they got into the boat to attend Mass on Gasparee. After that, they would spend the rest of the day at the uncle's house, beginning the day with Charles's father's famous rum punch, and eating Naomi's famous lemon and ginger kingfish. While the mothers, aunties and grannies prepared the meal, the fathers sat on the deck with coolers and kept a semi-vigilant eye on their children, nephews, nieces, cousins, and friends' children jumping off the deck, or driving the small whalers around the bay.

Charles and Robby never admitted it, but they knew in their hearts that it was not the costs involved in taking care of *Naomi* that made them want to sell the boat, it was more the difficulty of managing the memory of their father, as he drove her through the waters like the true captain he was, leaving beautiful roosters and the other boats behind. He was always cracking his five favourite jokes, followed by his booming laugh that was always funnier than the joke itself. Passing the rough waters of the three Bocas, he always reminded the boys that *boca* was mouth in Spanish. Then he would say one mouth to Tobago, one to Venezuela and one to God. By the time they dropped anchor in Scotland Bay, he had already opened the first of many cold beers. As boys, Charles and Robby would try to swim to shore to escape their father's Scotland Bay lectures, because with each beer he would expound, with less evidence but greater conviction, on any subject to the people on their boat, friends on other boats or to anyone he met in the bay. His themes invariably included the West Indies cricket team, which usually led to The West Indian Federation, which slid easily into the first President and finally onto the Water and Sewage Authority (their father was obsessed with clean waters, rivers and seas), and then to the overarching theme: the decline of the island. In the end, though, all topics found their way back to the art of fishing and Gerry Butcher's love of the sea.

After any of these down-the-islands trips, if the boat wasn't just moored but berthed, Charles' father would not let the workers in the club wash down the boat. If the boys were there, Gerry Butcher would always say, "No, thank you, my dear man. My boys will do it. It's good for them." His father always called the workers "Sir" or "My dear man", and he often told Charles and Robby that they should always remember to give those who were less fortunate greater respect than the fortunate fools who seldom deserved it.

Over the years Charles had spent less time down-the-islands and more time in the office doing the work of the boat insurance business he inherited from his father. Robby took charge of another part of the business, which followed more closely in their father's footsteps, purchasing boats, reselling to upgrade, running the tackle shop. He entered several fishing tournaments throughout the Caribbean, but never fared as well as his father. Robby also began to spend more time down-the-islands during the vacations and always took their mother there for Christmas and Easter. Naomi never missed an opportunity to tell Charles that Robby had truly taken over from his father.

★

Since his boyhood, Charles had always preferred the property in Blanchisseuse overlooking Marian's Bay, even though it was less spacious than the island home on Monos and more basic: Morris chairs, bunk beds, hammocks, white pine dining table and Adirondack chairs. The dishes, pots and pans were all things Naomi no longer wanted in their home in town, but still Charles preferred it. The Blanchisseuse house felt less restricted than the other homes, less ruled over by his parents – like living in a camp filled with all the possibilities of adventure.

Sometimes at night, bats would dart through the living room, especially if they left the large Demerara windows open too late into the evening. Naomi would scream at the sight of the small black creature shooting frantically around the room trying to escape, then rush into a bathroom or bedroom, lock the door and refuse to come out until Charles, Robby, Gerry and any other guests in the house, armed with mops and brooms, could assure her that the house was bat free. Charles's father would pretend that the broom was sword, an *epée*, (tossing around the little French he knew from his mother's side of the family) and shouting: "*En garde, en garde, diable*," as he took a sword fighter pose, making the boys crack up with laughter – something their mother could never find amusing.

The Blanchisseuse house had two verandahs, one at the front and the other at the back; the verandah at the back was long and wide, made of hard wood and filled with white wooden benches, thick round teak tables and several Adirondack chairs. It had a clear view of the Caribbean sea. From this verandah they faced a large rock in the sea often covered with sea gulls, frigate birds and pelicans. Their father called this rock *Diamant*, after a similar rock in Martinique, and the small town his mother's family was from. Charles still remembered his father taking Robby and himself as boys to meet their Martinican cousins. On that same vacation the entire clan from Trinidad and Martinique took a short boat trip to the diamond-shaped rock. At Blanchisseuse, when he and

79

Robby behaved particularly badly, their mother would threaten to leave them on the Diamant for the rest of the day. Two boys close in age must have been hard on their mother; Charles remembered how he and Robby would run up and down the back verandah, their feet loud on the wood, and try to hang over the edge of the wooden railing that jutted out just beyond the cliff where the waves crashed onto the rocks below. Their playful screams and those godforsaken bats must have made it impossible for Naomi to relax in that house, even though she tried; she knew how much Gerry and the boys loved the place.

Sometimes, Robby and Charles would sneak down the forbidden path below the back verandah that led to the rocks, where thick vines fell from the sea grape bushes and sea almond trees. Charles, who fancied himself as a Tarzan, would grab a vine or two, hoping to land on a rock below. He would often overestimate his brother Robby's loyalty and find his mother or father waiting for his return on the back verandah with a frown that meant he would have to spend the rest of the day inside.

Gerry Butcher cared much less about where they vacationed, and more about the amount of his time he could spend on his boat. As the children became teenagers and Blanchisseuse became again a popular spot, Naomi decided to renovate the house. The wood was replaced by whitewashed walls; the old Morris chairs and tables were exiled to the caretaker's cottage, replaced by beautiful rattan sofas and custom-made daybeds that lined the refurbished front porch; all of the bedrooms were air-conditioned; the old Demerara windows replaced with sliding glass and new Adirondack chairs were bought for the back verandah. Charles felt that the house had lost all its old character, but even though he preferred the old furniture and the noisy wooden verandah, the house still held centre-stage in the few memories he had of himself as a boy, the place where he had felt most secure.

The brothers never discussed how the properties should be divided after their father died. They seemed to be naturally drawn to different locations and if ever there were times when both families wanted the same house on the same dates each brother would concede to the other. Their father had told them too many tragic stories about families broken apart in bitter arguments over land and money. Charles remembered them and if Robby, the more businesslike of the two, ever forgot their father's lessons, Charles would give in to his younger brother, to avoid the vulgarity of arguing over money. There were times when his wife accused him of being weak; she felt that when it came to his family Charles had no backbone.

Charles's thoughts returned not only to the argument with his wife but to their marriage. He tried not to think about it too much, believing in his father's words that you had to take life as it came to you, like the sea. This philosophy may have worked with his father and mother, but it didn't work with Elena. Life with Elena could move too rapidly from dead calm to tsunami. His wife's unhappiness, he rationalized, was probably the result of her loneliness as an only child from a broken home. This was what his mother had told him when he and Elena were having terrible fights early in their marriage. Things had been better after that, but in the last few years Charles felt that his wife's irritability and sadness had returned; he could only point to Ruthie's leaving for university, her troubles in Boston, her pregnancy and their leaving the valley for San Pedro. Charles would have liked to fix all of these things but knew he could only try to live with them and avoid the arguments as much as possible.

After his lunch, Charles spent the rest of the afternoon busying himself with work he would normally assign to his secretaries and accountants: filing, reviewing the financial statements, looking at Robbie's sales in the tackle shop. At about three o'clock he took a short walk to the parlour next to the roti shop, bought a newspaper, a bottle of water and two nut cakes. On the way back he discarded what was left of his half-eaten shrimp roti in a dumpster at the back of his office. As he reopened his office door and sat behind his desk, it occurred to him that he did not want to go home.

★

Mrs. B felt extremely uneasy. Charles seldom left the house after an argument and the ease with which he had walked out troubled her. The house was empty now and very quiet. Ruthie had gone to the hotel pool earlier that morning with Monique. Mrs. B had no plans except the desire to call Larry again. She dialled his cell-phone number, because she was afraid of Rachel picking up the landline. Larry answered.

"Hi Larry. Sorry to bother you…" she said, "but I'm just checking to see if Charles is with you."

"You're never a bother. No, he's not with me. You lost your hubby?" Larry sounded friendly, as though the conversation about Monique had never taken place. That was Larry's way, always ready to move on, making life easier for himself.

"For the moment yes, but I'm sure he'll be back soon."

"So what you did to make the man run away?" He gave his boyish chuckle and Mrs. B imagined the dimpled smile.

"You wouldn't want to know; it's really foolish, childish."

"Childish? Coming from you, that's really surprising. So what did you accuse him of now?" Larry wanted to play with her. She lied that Charles was angry because she didn't want to play mas. She didn't mention the part about Monique.

"Why don't you want to play? I thought you said you had a grand time last year."

And that was the truth. Grand was the word. She had danced for two days, surviving on coconut water, scotch and soca; everyone said she looked beautiful and for the first time in years she believed it. But that was March, almost a month before Ruthie's breakdown.

"Ruthie, she's due around that time, give or take a week. I really don't want to be in the middle of the band while she's at home in labour. Anything could happen…"

"So don't play. Stay with Ruthie. Let Charles play and you can call him on his cell, that is unless he has it on vibrate, then again he might be vibrating on some hot young babe in the band." Larry laughed again.

"Yeah, thanks, Larry. Great idea." She laughed. "But just re-member, Charles is not into robbing the cradle like some people."

"So you think, Mrs. B, so you think."

"So I know."

"Listen, let the man play his mas and you stay at home like a good wife and take care of your one and only daughter. You know, we've gone over this many times before, you know where a woman's place is…"

"Yes I do, on the sofa in your office."

They both laughed. She knew that he would remember (or at least she hoped he would) their first time (now almost two decades ago) in his office one Sunday morning. Mrs. B's pulse raced; Larry was a master at flirtation, so to protect herself she cut the conversation short.

"Listen, gotta go. We'll talk."

"Well that was abrupt. Yes, that was a coitus, no sorry discussionus interruptus." Larry knew she liked his fake Latin. "Okay, Mrs. B, good luck finding Mr. B."

And that was it. Mrs. B put the receiver back down. She regretted the call, regretted giving into her weakness. Larry could always get her to flirt with him and she could never resist.

★

When Charles came home at five, he found an empty house. Elena's note said she had gone for a walk around the Savannah, and that was what she had intended to do, but at the traffic lights she had turned right and driven towards Chaguaramas. She'd passed the grand houses on the hills of Goodwood Park, passed the poorer ones in the village down below, passed the Yacht Club, the shopping centre, the fish depot in Carenage and the "Welcome to Chaguaramas" sign. Saw families bathing in shallow, dirty water at William's Bay. Did they know about the tests done on the water? Did they care? But the sea looked so inviting, flat, calm like a deep shimmering emerald; the temptation to jump in was evidently overpowering.

Mrs. B thought she would turn back at Bayside Restaurant where she'd had so many lunches with Kathy and Jackie, but she didn't. She kept driving until she got to the end of the road for civilians, facing the entrance into the coastguard base where the old hotel used to be. She remembered coming to this place once as a child with her parents. It was one of the few memories she had of them laughing together. The guard in the booth waved to her; no civilians were allowed beyond this point. She turned the SUV around in the empty car park and headed towards home. But then she stopped at the marina where Charles's family had their two boats. The thought crossed her mind to ask Sugars, one of the boatmen in the Marina, to take her across to the house on Monos.

It would be empty since Robby was away on business and even if he had lent it to friends for the weekend, she could make up some excuse when she got there. She turned into the marina parking lot, took her bag, cell phone and membership card, remembered to lock the doors, set the alarm button on her key chain and crossed the empty street.

The marina was quiet. Most of the island homeowners would have gone down on Friday evening or early Saturday morning to get in two full days. She inquired about Sugars who looked after their boat; one of the attendants, an older man whose face she knew but whose name always escaped her, told her that he had just taken some people over to Scotland Bay and would be back soon. The man had obviously recognized her and asked if Mr. Charles would need the boat. Mrs. B told him that it was just her, that she needed to get something from the house. They made a little small talk; the weather had been dry and windy, the waves high and the water rough. "But today it's as flat as glass, like a mirror," he said.

Standing on the deck, waiting for Sugars, Mrs. B had no idea why she was going down to the house without Charles; it was something she had never done in their entire marriage. But then she spotted the white pirogue approaching, with Sugars handling the boat with casual expertise. She tried her best to look purposeful as the boat docked.

Sugars did not get out of the boat, but stuck his head to one side, his huge golden afro sparkling in the sun, and called out to one of the boys on the jetty to help him tie up the boat. He had two passengers with him, a middle-aged white American man and a young local dougla girl who had been sitting on the man's lap, but got off when Sugars called out to the boys. She wore a tight orange tube top that barely held her huge breasts and displayed her nipples; her short shorts revealed part of her bottom and a tattoo of a huge snake on her upper thigh; there was another snake on her upper arm. Mrs. B thought she recognized the man but she wasn't sure because he made his way past her very quickly, barely helping the young girl off the boat.

The older attendant approached, just as Mrs. B was about to talk to Sugars, who now stood on the jetty, being paid by the

American. The girl held a basket with an empty bottle of rum and some coke cans. Some of the young boys in the yard were calling out to the girl; they seemed to know her.

"Sugars, you have one more trip today, boy," the old man said. "The Mrs. need to go down to Mr. Charles house."

"No problem, Mr. Mac. It still early. One trip or two?" Sugars, out of respect, did not put the question to Mrs. B although she was close by. The older man turned to her; his name was Mr. MacKenzie, she remembered now.

"I just need to get something at the house, just to go down and come back up; it shouldn't take long. Mr. Charles had to work today and Mr. Robert is not in the country." Mrs. B was not sure why she felt the need to explain this to Mr. Mac and Sugars.

"No problem, Miss Charles," Mr. Mac said. "That's all you have, nothing else to put on?"

"That's it. Just me," she said.

"Sugars, Miss Charles waiting," Mr. Mac said, turning away from Mrs. B.

Sugars was having an intense discussion with a thin Indian boy, who had been calling out to the girl on the jetty. Mrs. B thought that the conversation had something to do with the American and the girl who had just come off the boat. "Doh ask me to do that again," was the last thing she heard Sugars say.

The crossing was not rough at all. Mrs. B looked out past Centipede Island, towards the Boca. The day was very clear, and she imagined she could see the shape of mountains towards Venezuela, but knew they were too far away. Sugars, usually quite talkative, was silent, as far away in his thoughts as Mrs. B was in hers. She surmised that the trip with the American and the girl had soured his mood in some way. As they approached the house he pulled alongside the deck, jumped off and tied up. Sugars held out his hand as he helped Mrs. B off the boat.

"Thank you," she said.

"What time for the trip back this afternoon, Miss Charles?"

"I'll be here for an hour or so." She reached in her bag for her wallet. Normally she went across in one of the family boats; she had no idea what a trip across to the house should cost. "How much for the trip?"

"No charge, Miss Charles. Old man Butcher pay for all this a long time ago." Mrs. B knew that Sugars meant Charles's father, not Charles himself. Old man Butcher had spent a lot of time in the marina. It was a second home, with evenings spent liming on the bench near to the jetty, buying beers for Sugars and Mac who had worked on the jetty as young teenagers, perhaps even younger than the new group of boys there now.

As Sugars turned and drove the boat away, she noticed that he was going a lot faster; the rooster tail was much higher than when they crossed. He would probably make it back in half the time.

Turning towards the house, she saw Blacks, the caretaker, coming towards her. Blacks was no longer called Blacks. He had a Muslim name now but she couldn't remember was it was. He looked rumpled, as though he had been taking a siesta and had suddenly been awoken to find his boss's wife standing on the lower deck. Usually if Charles or his brother were coming down, they would call Blacks on his cell phone to let him know to open up the house and make sure that everything was in order.

"Sorry, Miss Charles, I didn't know you was making a trip today." He was still trying to tidy himself up, tucking his white vest into his old khaki shorts that Mrs. B recognized having given it to him when they no longer fitted Charles. Blacks and Charles had been about the same height and size at one time, but while Charles's waist and paunch had increased, Blacks had remained very trim. He had always been a good worker; he had been with the family now for the last seven years, having taken over from his uncle who used to work for Gerry Butcher. Whenever the family was at the house, Blacks, who no longer ate meat, would offer the family his famous fish broth made with cassava, yam, dasheen, dumplings and kingfish or carite and his delicious coconut bake. Blacks, with his smooth deep blue skin, reminded Mrs. B of Sidney Poitier. She and Jackie had always found Blacks quite beautiful. One look at Blacks and Jackie would say, "Delicious, simply delicious."

"No, I didn't know I was coming down today. I just decided I needed to get something from the house." Mrs. B was now explaining everything to Blacks. All he was supposed to do was open up for her and help her with anything she needed.

As they walked up the steps, she noticed quite a few empty beers on the table in the pagoda next to the small jacuzzi that Robby had built. Blacks saw her look across and felt, as a good Muslim, he had to explain.

"They left the beers there last night. Mr. Chin had a party for his daughter, eighteenth birthday party. I think some of them swam across on this side." Blacks said he planned to wash down the deck today. He seemed a little nervous about the beers, but Mrs. B wasn't paying much attention to the excuse or to the fact that there was a pair of lady-size flip-flops next to the deck chair by the jacuzzi.

The house was divided into three levels. The first was a general living and cooking area with a bedroom and bathroom; the second and third levels were for the family; Mrs. B and Charles, who seldom came down to the house, were on the top level; Robby, his family and Naomi were on the larger second level. Each level had three large bedrooms, two bathrooms and a living area that flowed onto another deck looking onto the bay.

Mrs. B had last come down to the house after her trip to Boston. She remembered spending a day on the deck with Charles. She remembered how sad they were about their daughter and how little they spoke about it. Since Ruthie's return they had not come down. Every time Robby or Naomi had invited them to the house, she had made excuses, citing Ruthie's pregnancy. This was not too far from the truth. Ruthie had said quite clearly that she did not want to be "put on display" for the family and Mrs. B could not argue with that. She knew that the family would be making judgments, evaluating Ruthie's psychological condition even more than her physical one.

She noticed that Robby had bought new furniture for his deck and that there was a lovely daybed at the far end. She told Blacks that the place looked good.

"The gardeners only coming down two Fridays a month now, so I have to keep up the place." He seemed pleased that she had noticed how manicured the plant beds looked.

When Blacks opened the door to her level, there was a musty smell; Blacks had obviously not dusted it in a while. Everything was tidy and in its place, but as Mrs. B put her bag on the table it felt slightly greasy with a layer of dust and sea grime covering everything. Blacks opened the doors to the deck and put out some of the deck chairs that had been stored in one of the bedrooms; he went to the small kitchenette and got out some Lysol and a cloth, wiped the chairs, put out the cushions and carried a small table onto the deck.

"Don't do too much. I'm not staying long," she said, walking over to small fridge to see what was in it.

"No problem, Miss Charles," Blacks said, continuing with his work on the deck. "I'll go downstairs and turn on the water pump."

There was nothing unrecognizable in the fridge: ketchup, Dijon mustard, chutneys, pepper sauce, and everything else that they did not want to leave for the ants in the small pantry: sugar, coffee, even the bottle of salt. There were always a couple of Britta jugs – Charles was obsessive about clean water (like his father) – there was also a filter on the sink taps. Mrs. B took out a bottle of gin and tonic water from the fridge and mixed a strong drink and then, as though in a trance, she walked onto the deck and sat on the slightly damp chair that looked out onto the bay. She had told Sugars to come back in an hour but now she knew she was going to stay. After her second drink, she called Charles, told him where she was and that she would not be home until the next day. All he said was "Okay."

# PART TWO

# CHAPTER ONE
## ANTS – TRINIDAD JANUARY 2010

On the same day that Ruthie lost Maria they found the serial killer in Manzanilla. The man known as "The Butcher" was sighted at the back of the community centre on Point Mitan Road; he was filling a plastic bottle with rusty tap water when a little boy and his mother spotted him. The Butcher ran as soon as he locked eyes with the little boy, who was staring at him. The mother stood motionless because she too recognized the man from the photos in the newspaper that clearly showed the thick, long scars on both cheeks. Since Ruthie's return, the Butcher had killed twelve people, most recently a mother and son. His method was always the same, he decapitated his victims, amputated their feet at the ankles, and scattered the body parts in refuse dumps throughout the island. The next day the newspapers had the Butcher's capture on the front page; he had thrown himself into the bushes, leaving his bottle of water behind, but the brave little boy had run faster than the wind in the opposite direction towards a police van he had seen higher up the road. The officers had stopped to buy homemade coconut ice cream. With the Butcher's capture, the nation breathed a sigh of relief, but Ruthie could only think about Maria.

★

About two weeks later, at seven o'clock on a Monday morning Ruthie had just finished her walk around the Queen's Park Savannah. It took her half an hour to get around. She started at Queen's Royal College and usually ended at the Archbishop's residence. On weekday mornings, the traffic was backed-up for miles; cars were filled with yawning parents and half-asleep children who had got up in the dark just to make it to school on time. Ruthie could have been one of those mothers. She imagined herself in the car with Maria at four, six, twelve and even a fresh, beautiful sixteen. These thoughts were too painful. They served no purpose now. They only prolonged the pain, stabbed at the fresh wound, so she shooed them away like a nagging fly.

Ruthie would have walked around again but the sun was beating down on her. Most of the runners and walkers were leaving as well; only crazy American tourists, or British expats started their exercise routine in this fiery air. It was Monique who had made Ruthie start these morning walks. Mrs. B thought that Ruthie needed more time to recover, but Ruthie didn't want time to recover. How much rest did an un-pregnant or ex-pregnant mother need? Once the bleeding had stopped, lying in bed with suffocating thoughts was dangerous, more dangerous than a walk around the Savannah. Ruthie knew that her thoughts had led her into the bathroom in Boston. Her thoughts had taken the pills out of the medicine cabinet, and the rest was history.

Monique's solution to any problem in life began with drinking coconut water on a bench at the Savannah; the Savannah had healing powers, and an early morning walk could cure sadness, sometimes even madness. But Ruthie had to walk alone now that Monique could no longer join her; she had found a job in her uncle's firm. She needed the money to move out of her parents' house, to get away from their constant surveillance.

Before Ruthie left the Savannah, she would turn away from the busy road and face the sprawling samaan trees in the middle of the wide green landscape. She loved to gaze at these trees before she left. As she looked down at her dirty sneakers, she noticed a line of black ants following a zigzag path across the blades of dry grass and fallen brown leaves. At first, the ants' route seemed to lead nowhere, but then she saw a discarded box of fried chicken that didn't quite make the dustbin and knew then that these red ants had a goal.

There had been a fat, brown, middle-aged lady with a short Afro living in the Savannah when Ruthie and Monique first began their morning walks. They would see her bathing under one of the pipes in a loose dress, washing her folds of flesh very carefully, not afraid to expose her body for the sake of cleanliness;

she even washed her sheets and used the lower branches of a tree like a line. One day, Ruthie and Monique noticed that the lady had disappeared. A coconut cart vendor told them that she had been beaten and raped by another vagrant. One night, the police found her bleeding on her bench and the authorities took her to the mental hospital at St. Ann's. But Ruthie still looked for her every morning, hoping she would reappear. She recognized many of the vagrants now: the semi-homeless, the sane-homeless, the filthy-homeless, the drunken-homeless, the druggie-homeless and, worst of the lot, the aged-homeless. They slept on benches at different locations around the Savannah. Depending on how early Ruthie began her morning walk, many of them would still be asleep, lying on the benches on their sides or backs, stiff as statues as though frozen overnight. Later in the morning, when the sun rose high enough for them to feel its light and heat, they would begin to pack up whatever they had used to cover themselves: old sheets, old clothes, rags, flattened cardboard boxes. In the beginning, just walking past one of them on a bench would make Ruthie nauseous, but now she could tolerate the stinking body odours and even perversely enjoy the stench.

★

In January, the weather was windy and dry. Maria *was* due in mid to late February, close to Carnival. Maria *is* due assumed a future, but is had become was. Maria was now no more than a simple past, a preterite Maria. Thinking of these changes, present to future, future to *passé composé* did not help Ruthie at all. Maria Lucia Butcher was the name she had chosen. Perhaps it had been bad luck to give the baby a name before she had come into this world; she had put goat mouth on the child – and knowing the name added to the pain. She saw life now, her life, through a veil of mourning for her Maria.

Two nights before Ruthie lost Maria she had a dream. It was a dream about Haitians. It was a dream she had a week before the world lost generations of Haitians, before the earthquake buried them. In the dream Ruthie was on the tarmac, about to board a plane to leave somewhere. It was not her home, it was not Haiti (though she has never been to Haiti), it was not Boston or New York, but somewhere else, maybe another island. Before she began to go up the steps to the plane she turned to see a group of people standing behind glass doors. She knew they were Haitians. At first, she thought they were waving at her, but then, as she looked closer, she saw that they were hitting the glass doors, they were suffocating. She never told anyone about this dream. She thought it arose from her anxiety about the horrible pain she would have during labour, and from a book she was reading about the Nazis, called *The Book Thief*. She had replaced Jews with Haitians, but only much later realized that the dream was there to warn her about the singular, personal, and collective pain that was about to crack, shake or shatter the faith of so many – for losing generations of families, for losing a single baby.

★

After their morning walks, Monique and Ruthie would drive to a popular doubles' vendor known as Captain, his stand just minutes away from the Savannah. He was always dressed in the white uniform, white sneakers and the Admiral's cap he had inherited from his father, Admiral, who had long since retired. He wore plastic gloves over the white ones to avoid the yellow stain from the curry. It was strange that while most strong smells still made Ruth nauseous, for some reason she could eat curry. She craved goat roti from a particular roti shop in St. James and doubles from Captain.

Ruthie and her father had always loved doubles. When she was at high school, they would stop for doubles every morning he took her. Her mother did not approve of curry for breakfast; she usually prepared bacon, eggs and buttered toast. So if her mother was dropping her to school, Ruthie knew not to ask to stop for doubles. When they lived in the valley, Ruthie and her father would pull into the parking lot where Admiral had his stand, the warm bara covered with a cloth and two white buckets – one filled with channa and the other with special mixture of peppers, cucumbers and tambran sauce. In a smaller container, he had the mango chutney. Ruthie and her father always had the same order. Admiral, recognizing the car, would start to prepare the order: three doubles, two with "slight" pepper for Charles and one with mango chutney, no pepper, for Ruthie.

★

It was now almost March, three months since Ruthie lost Maria. A drought had been declared throughout the Caribbean – St Lucia, Grenada, Antigua and even lush Dominica – the islands were suffering, praying for rain. The hills were burnt black and dust covered everything: hair, clothes, plants and cars. At night, above the black hills, the sky was orange with the flames, the air was filled with smoke.

The government threatened fines for anyone caught using their sprinklers, but never actually fined anyone, though armed patrols were sent when water trucks went into the poorer villages. On the Savannah, the grass got browner, but the President's palace lawn remained deep green.

Ruthie remembered that when she was a young girl the valley would glow from all the fires. She would be afraid to go outside, fearing that the fires would suddenly rage through the bamboo on their property and in minutes she too would be ablaze. Worse still were the drives from school in the hot afternoons when the fires from the hills reached the valley road and the flames would lick the side of her father's car.

This year the yellow poui trees flowered for a shorter time than normal because of the extraordinarily dry season; a few pink pouis bloomed leaving their delicate pink carpets on the paved walkway around the Savannah. The carpets lightened Ruthie's spirits for a moment, but she was careful not to allow herself to indulge for too long in these small pleasures. Life played horrible tricks on you, especially if you started to believe that any joy could last. Happiness was a dangerous indulgence.

★

Mrs. B did not know how to deal with the loss of Maria and for some reason she saw herself as responsible for this tragedy. Not Ruthie, not Charles, not her absentee parents, not her great aunts, not the President, not the Professor, not the nursing home, not the doctors, not even Monique. Mrs. B had decided that she was liable, accountable, definitely the one to blame and all she could feel was guilt. She had committed the one offence that she had tried to avoid. She was a bad mother, perhaps even worse than her own. At least Simone had not made any pretence of being a good mother or of having a daughter who would add to her list of accomplishments. Mrs. B had wanted Ruthie to shine, and even outshine those around her, but she had failed. Mrs. B had managed to suppress Ruthie's episode in Boston, she had tried to disregard the affair with the married professor (Ruthie had finally told them about the whole sordid affair). She had even been able to cope with the public humiliation of an unmarried pregnant daughter. As Kathy and Jackie said, times had changed, and so many girls now had children out of wedlock – and gave examples of this family and that one. Still, Mrs. B was no fool. Which mother looked forward to a daughter in this condition, twenty-first century or not? In a place as small as this, shame could hit you in the grocery, at the mall, at the hair salon, even at dinner with friends. Every time someone who knew about Ruthie's loss said they were sorry about what had happened, or even looked at Mrs. B with pity, a feeling of shame took over her. It often took days to recover from one of these encounters.

And yet, despite this stew of shame, guilt, responsibility and blame, Mrs. B resented Ruthie for revealing what a bad mother she was – even though she knew that this resentment was what made her feel like a bad mother in the first place. Mrs. B had spent a good deal of time criticizing and judging mothers who had neglected their children for their careers; she had found enthusiastic support for these pronouncements from her friends Kathy and Jackie, who had also never pursued any job that would take them away from their family. Those in their circle who did – the female lawyers, doctors, professors, accountants and, the worst of the lot, the female corporate executives – faced harsh disapproval from Mrs. B, especially if she felt able to point to how badly their children were doing in school. These children needed more attention from their parents and by parents, she meant the mothers not the fathers. The mothers were selfish and vain to let their children fall behind while they shone in their careers. Ruthie had been Mrs. B's proof of self-sacrifice and success. And if the children of these working mothers managed to beat the competition, Mrs. B would point to some other defect in the family – an unhappy husband or a dysfunctional marriage. Kathy and Jackie never disagreed with these assessments.

Mrs. B was angry, irritated, irritable about everything and

nothing in particular; this anger showed itself most at dinner time, the big meal of the day since Charles was seldom at home for lunch. Mrs. B would lay the table with the meal Milly had prepared; she would call Charles and Ruthie and then absent herself, with the excuse that she had already eaten or she was not feeling well. Charles and Ruthie knew better than to complain about her absence, and, to be honest, dinner was always easier without Mrs. B at the table. The few times she sat with them she spent the entire meal criticizing the way Milly had overcooked the roast or undercooked the potatoes. She begged Ruthie to use a knife and avoid eating in that horrible American way. But if she was a bad mother, was there anything she could do about it?

## CHAPTER TWO
## POOLSIDE

Monique looked frazzled. She had obviously been crying. Her make-up was a mess, with raccoon eyes and smears of red lipstick around her mouth. Her thick hair, normally pulled into a fairly neat bun, was loose and strands were covering part of her face. She called the number again but this time there was no response. Calling herself a fuckingidiotfuckingidiotfuckingidiot, she texted something, sent it, texted again, sent it, and all the while Ruthie looked on from her deck chair. They were poolside at the hotel.

Monique had come to there to have lunch with Ruthie. Ruthie knew who she was calling, knew the whole story. Monique had told her everything on their last drive home from Maracas. It was about the affair that she was having with an older married man, someone both their parents knew. Monique and Ruthie also knew the children in the family and now the man had decided to end it all after having promised Monique a trip to London and money towards a new car.

"I am sucking up to an asshole, begging a fucking pig not to leave me. Can you even believe that?" Monique had almost finished her scotch and coconut water.

"Would you believe me when I say yes?" Both smiled. They believed they knew exactly what the other was feeling, although Monique also thought that at least she hadn't got pregnant. Ruthie was thinking the same thing.

"That family is so frigging strange. I mean the son is the shortest idiot on the planet and the daughters look like they have definitely suffered some kind of abuse. One is anorexic for sure and the other is bordering on obese." Ruthie stuffed her mouth with some more fries.

"Well, thanks friend, that really helps." Monique kept her eye on her cell phone. She wasn't angry or even irritated; none of what Ruthie said mattered right now. All she wanted was to hear from him, saying he wanted her back in his life.

Then finally a text; he could meet her tonight to talk. Ruthie was curious, even a little envious of a rendezvous like the ones she used to have with her Professor.

"He has a place near to the warehouse in Arima."

"A hook-up in a warehouse in Arima? How romantic."

"Not in the warehouse close to… Anyway stop being such a fucking snob, better than an office desk."

"Okay, now we're even."

The text reply had put Monique just slightly more at ease; she had one more scotch and coconut water, barely ate any of her burger and fries, and said she had to leave. Ruthie resumed the book she was reading by a writer she had met once at a conference with her Professor – Danny Laferrière's *How to make love to a Negro without getting tired.*

★

Mrs. B had only visited Aunt Claire three times since Ruthie had returned; these quick visits were mainly to help her aunt with money matters. Claire had always seemed to manage well on her own, but recently she had begun to worry about her financial situation. Claire herself wondered if the worry was simply due to getting older, or the increase in burglaries in her neighbourhood (one of her neighbours had been beaten with a cutlass and robbed of the several thousand dollars he had just taken out of the bank for a weekend in Tobago). So for these reasons, and perhaps others she hadn't thought about yet, she had called on her niece a little more often than in the past.

Still, there were things in Claire's life that brought her some satisfaction. At the age of seventy she had finally managed to become a librarian, even though it was a primary school library, at the same primary school where she had taught for thirty-five years. Although she had imagined herself in the National Library surrounded by books on all subjects and strange new disciplines, rather than cataloguing Hardy Boys, Nancy Drew, Harry Potter, treasuries of fairy tales, or Roald Dahl, it was still a library. The primary school principal, a dear man called Mr. Sweet, had asked her to help in the library after she stopped teaching, and she had welcomed the opportunity to fill her day with something that took her out of the house. She had stopped doing volunteer work at the church since the new parish priest, Father Chin, seemed more concerned with raising money than gathering lost souls. But Father Chin was not the only reason. Claire had become less and less moved by her religion, even though time was on death's side. Life was not infinite, friends died or were beginning to die and with each loss, Claire lost a little bit of faith, sure that she would never see them again. She still went to church every Sunday morning. Sometimes, she still took two ninety-year old spinster sisters to the Saturday afternoon Mass, but all of this was more ritual than faith. The guilts that had punished her for so long grew lighter, and her new agnosticism had also helped her to let go of all the resentments, jealousy and anger that made any relationship with her sister Simone impossible. Now Simone's words, even across oceans of water, no longer poisoned Claire with bile. She had come to recognise that for a long time she had envied her sister's ability to free herself from everything that had been expected of her, including motherhood. She, on the other hand, who had tried to follow the family codes so carefully, had been the one to disappoint the family.

Looking back now she was grateful to her sister for those years with Marie Elena; it had brought her back to life, given her a purpose, as the library job was doing now.

Mrs. B did not know why she felt the need to visit her Aunt Claire that morning. She had no excuse and Claire had made no request: no bank cheque to deposit, no health insurance form to help her complete, but Mrs. B drove there anyway having turned down Charles's invitation to spend a day with Robby and family down-the-islands.

Claire came to the door dressed in a faded flowery house dress and the Birkenstock sandals that Mrs. B had given her for her last birthday. She looked a little surprised to see her niece at the doorstep. Mrs. B thought her aunt looked a little thinner than normal, but her face and beautiful skin seemed to glow. She certainly didn't look her age; Mrs. B recalled what the old aunts always said about Claire – that she had "good bones". They embraced and went out to the small porch. Mrs. B noticed the pile of books on the dining-room table.

Claire explained. "What I do is write a short paragraph about an interesting part or character in the new books that we get. They photocopy it in the office and pass it on to the children. I don't know if it helps encourage the children to read, probably not. But if I get even one or two more students borrowing a book during the week, I'm happy. Two types of people you know: the readers and nonreaders; the only problem is the nonreaders rule the world." Claire smiled and looked directly into her niece's eyes.

"Well, Auntie, maybe you're right; we aren't all readers. Ruthie has always been more of a reader than me. I think I'm somewhere in between – or maybe it just depends on how busy I am."

Claire made her a cup of coffee and offered her a poppy seed muffin. Mrs. B accepted the muffin out of politeness but only nibbled at it.

Mrs. B wanted to confide in her aunt but did not know where to begin. Claire knew about the miscarriage. She knew about Ruthie's affair, she knew about Ruthie's suicide attempt in Boston. But Mrs. B was not there to talk about any of these things and yet all of these things seemed to have led her to where she was in her life, sitting on her Aunt Claire's back porch facing the hills she had not seen, or rather had not noticed, in such a long time.

"There are so many houses there now; I remember when I was younger the hills were just green. Some parts look scarred, so ugly."

"I guess I've just got used to them. They don't bother me that much any more, though with all the fires they look much worse." Claire sipped her tea then added a little more sugar.

"How is the library going? I keep forgetting to bring that book I promised you. Next time I'll remember."

"Not to worry; you have given so many books already, Elena, more than some of the parents. They don't seem to care about whether their kids read or not. All they seem to care about is new technology. What does that matter if they can't read?"

"I guess technology... all of that is important now. It's not like before." Mrs. B sipped her coffee.

101

"No, it's not like before, but what do they say? *Plus ça change plus c'est la même chose,* but if they can't read… Anyway it doesn't matter."

"We have to change with the times. We can't go back, Auntie."

"Maybe it's just me getting old. Sometimes I wonder why I try with my silly little summaries. I'm sure very soon they'll stack me up like the old chairs at the back of the school." But these words, Mrs. B felt, were not said with hopelessness or resignation, but uttered with a fighting spirit. How was it that Aunt Claire seemed to be getting stronger in her old age whilst she felt herself getting weaker?

"I'm thinking of going away for a while," Mrs. B said, without looking directly at her aunt.

"Are you and Charles going on vacation?"

"No, just me. I haven't said anything to Charles as yet. It's still an idea."

"That's good, a little break for yourself. Where will you go? You could visit your parents in Ft. Lauderdale."

"No I don't think so. The last visit was such a disaster, I don't think I want to do that again, at least not now. I think Ruthie has been in touch, but sometimes you have to protect yourself from Simone." Mrs. B could not believe that she had actually said those words to her Aunt. Simone had said and done horrible things to them both over the years, but they had never said what they both felt, at least not directly.

"Yes, Simone doesn't change. But I know she loves you, Lena."

Mrs. B didn't answer. She had never been convinced of that; there seemed very little to support the idea.

"How is Ruthie doing?"

"Okay I guess. You know Ruthie. She's very private, quiet, doesn't say much to me. She talks a little more with her father."

Mrs. B knew that Claire thought that she was planning her break because of what had happened to Ruthie, but that was only a very small part of it.

"Maybe if she gets a job that will help. She could write for the newspapers, or teach." Claire was not sure about what she should say to her niece, who seemed so far away from where they were actually sitting.

"I don't think she wants to do anything. I guess she'll do something in her own time. It's hard. When you come back, jobs aren't waiting for you any more." But Mrs. B knew that wasn't the case with Ruthie; she hadn't even tried to find a job. Charles had offered to talk to friends, but Ruthie said she wasn't ready. Neither Mrs. B nor Charles wanted to force her; they were always afraid of what Ruthie might do if she became overly stressed.

"Ruthie will find her way," Claire said, without completely believing it. "Have you thought about where you want to go?"

"Go where?"

"Your vacation, have you thought about where?"

"Yes, yes, I have a few ideas. It may not be too far, maybe just another island, maybe New York, I don't know yet; all I know is that I need a little time away." What Mrs. B really wanted to say was *run away*.

"We get to that point sometimes, don't we? When we feel we just need to step back and look on, just for a little bit."

"Yes," Mrs. B said, "that's what I want to do, just look on for a little while."

The conversation ended on the safer topic of politics. The President for some bizarre reason (bizarre even for him) had decided to call an election before the end of his term. He was convinced that the opposition, which had been squabbling and exposing their dirty laundry in public, would get a drubbing. He was alleged to have said he would crush every last one of them like ants. Neither Claire nor Mrs. B cared much for politics, but they spoke as though they did, since neither wanted to continue talking about personal matters. Mrs. B's visit left Claire with an uneasy feeling; she did not sleep well that night.

★

When Mrs. B got home she found an empty house. Charles would probably be gone until late evening; the down-the-islands family limes with Robby and his friends seldom ended early. In the kitchen Mrs. B saw Ruthie's note on the fridge: "Gone to a film with Monique, see you later." Mrs. B did not want to lose the courage she had found at her aunt's home. She called her travel agent and found out the cost of return trips to New York, London, Aruba and Martinique. She spent the rest of the day researching the hotel costs for a month's stay in these places. There were so many options she began to feel dizzy and realized that she had not eaten a proper meal that day.

By evening, after a light meal, a glass of white wine and a shower, she had decided on Martinique. She knew it well, she was sure her French was passable and she, like Charles, had distant family on the island. She would leave on the 5th of May and be back by May 30th. Not quite a month, but it was what she could afford and she thought it would give her enough time to regain the energy to re-enter her life on her return. The greatest difficulty she faced now was telling Charles. He was under the illusion that they were happy again, reliving a second or even third honeymoon. She had given him reason to think this way; instead of playing Carnival, they had decided to go to Tobago. Neither could face Carnival after Ruthie lost the baby. They tried to persuade Ruthie to come with them and she had agreed until the very last day when she changed her mind. Ruthie really didn't see why at her age and having lived abroad for four years, she could not manage without her parents for four days. But Charles, even more than his wife, insisted that she stay with Grandmother Naomi. After several intense discussions and uncomfortable silences they agreed, with Naomi's consent, that Naomi would have to be discommoded to stay with her granddaughter. Though Naomi might have sounded slightly irritated with Charles, that was only from habit; in truth she loved the idea of spending time with Ruthie while her parents were away.

Mrs. B and Charles had rented a wooden bungalow in the fishing village of Charlotteville, which had uninterrupted views of the bay and the lush green hills at the back of the house. They had romantic dinners in the restaurant at the bottom of the hill and made love three times in the four days. An amazing feat for them. Sun, sea and rum punch had done the trick and Charles returned from the Tobago trip full of gusto and a renewed passion for life and sex with his wife. It was not the same for Mrs. B. She had certainly enjoyed their night-time escapades in the gigantic four-poster bed, with the mosquito netting adding more mystery and romance to the whole experience, but by the time she walked into the San Pedro condo the magic was gone. When Charles wanted to make love the night of their return she claimed to be too tired. Charles asked how she could be tired after a twenty-minute flight; she said it was the long drive from Charlotteville to the airport that had worn her down. Still, Charles seemed to have stored enough happiness from the Tobago trip to last him quite a while, enough contentment not to notice that his wife had quickly returned to the place they had left behind.

★

Call it serendipity, coincidence, karma, kismet or chance, but while Mrs. B was planning to leave the island, the Professor was planning to visit it. He would be in Cuba for a conference and suggested to Ruthie in an email that he could come and visit her for a few days. Ruthie said nothing to her parents about this; they thought that the relationship was in the buried past, especially with the loss of Maria. What Mrs. B and Charles did not know was that Ruthie and her Professor had been Facebooking, emailing and Skyping once again. Ruthie had called him soon after she lost Maria. Wanting to make him feel a hellish, suicidal guilt, she told him the ugliest things she could think of. She even threatened to slit her wrists this time, saying the blood would be on his hands etc… But Ruthie was also hoping that the Professor would do exactly what he was planning to do now, visit her and become part of her life again. She had imagined her Professor here with her so many times before that now she could hardly think about anything else; the visit was planned for what the Professor called "the spring".

"We have no spring here," she had teased him. "This is an island. We have two seasons, rain and less rain."

"I wish you would come back," he said.

"Come back where?"

"Come back to Boston, to Cambridge."

"Why?" she said.

"Because I miss you and I am sorry, really."

"Sorry for what?"

"Sorry for everything that has happened to you, Ruthie." The Professor said this in a voice that Ruthie did not easily recognize. He sounded sad. And this pleased her, softening some of her hardness and anger.

Charles noticed that Ruthie's mood was lighter, but he never asked why. He didn't know how long it would take for his daughter to get over the miscarriage, and he didn't know how to help her. He also noticed that his wife had regained her Tobago spirit and was more willing now to make love on a Saturday night. With the two women in his life in good moods, Charles had not felt so contented in years.

# CHAPTER THREE
## MENDACITY

The next two weeks were filled with events both in the nation and in the Butcher household. For the first time in a long time, Ruthie and her mother had something in common: they were both keeping a secret. The President also revealed his ill-kept secret. On the same day that Mrs. B finally confirmed both hotel in Martinique and ticket to leave Piarco, through Castries and then on to Fort de France, the President confirmed that there was to be a snap election.

It was during the week of the election announcement that the Professor emailed his itinerary to Ruthie. He would stay in Havana for five days, and then fly to Trinidad (via Miami) where he would spend the next five days before returning to Boston. Ruthie had suggested that he stay at the hotel where she had her pool and tennis court membership. This would be a perfect place for them to meet, especially since she had seldom seen anyone she knew at the pool, and even if she came across one or two while the Professor was there, it wouldn't seem strange for her to be seen talking to a tourist at the hotel pool – sneaking into his room would be a little trickier. She had also booked a room for two nights at a guest house on the north coast, recommended to her by Monique (the only one who knew about the Professor's visit). Ruthie wanted the Professor to see other parts of the island, not just the Savannah and Port of Spain. The beauties of the coast line and the wide beaches were all part of her itinerary for the Professor's visit. The secret planning brought back feelings of excitement, anticipation and a renewed sense of purpose – as though a part of her life had been given back to her. Now her mornings didn't always begin with thoughts of Maria.

Mrs. B had managed to keep her plans secret. Apart from her initial conversation with Aunt Claire and her travel agent, no one else knew. But she had decided that this was the week to tell Charles about her decision; she would also tell Jackie and Kathy. She would say she needed a break, blame it all on the stress with Ruthie; she did not plan to tell Ruthie any more than her itinerary.

★

At 2.15 pm, on an extraordinarily sunny afternoon, the President announced his list of candidates for the upcoming general election. It was replayed on all the radio stations at hourly intervals throughout the day. His familiar drone relayed to the nation who their new representatives would be, as if the opposition party did not exist and the elections were a mere formality. There had been no party council to decide who should represent them; according to rumour, the President had simply sent one of his security officers with a list of all the representatives to the party secretary. There were few surprises; the old guard would serve for the umpteenth time. But then came the last name on the list. The President paused, then announced that Mr. Lawrence Blackburn, of Blackburn and Mills Construction Development Co. Ltd. was to represent the North West.

By 2:33 pm, the northwestern circles to which Lawrence "Chow" Blackburn belonged were in frenzy. On mobile lines, land lines, text lines and people standing in line, they talked quietly but excitedly about the announcement. They could not understand how Chow could join a party that so few of his friends openly supported, even though at election time Chow's business friends would give gifts to ensure post-election favours, for one contract or another. None of them saw it as a bribe; it was just the way things were done. But none of his friends would ever think of joining the party. Friend and foe alike were curious and rumours flew faster than a speeding bullet. Friend and foe knew that Chow was a ruthless, unscrupulous developer, who had made millions (billions some said) building unsound high-rise high-end condominiums with cheap materials. These were for the up-and-coming, aspiring, just-arriving Black and Indian middle class. No one in Chow's circle bought a townhouse or condominium from Chow, but quite a few had invested in his developments. If Chow became

Minister of Housing, just think of the money he could make. He would no longer have to pass extra money to cut corners; he would own the corner. The second rumour, which resurfaced from the past, was a little less flattering. The Blackburn family owned three large properties down-the-islands: Belle Mer, Beau Séjour and Paradiso. Seven years ago there was a suspicious fire that burnt the original Beau Séjour to the ground, along with two police officers and the property caretaker. The rumour was that the police officers were there to collect drugs that had been left at the Blackburn house by Venezuelan drug dealers. Something had gone wrong with the exchange (the rumour never explained this part of the story) and the drug-dealing policemen were killed and then burnt in the fire along with the caretaker. The crime was investigated for about two minutes and then filed. Those in Chow's circle placed all the blame on the caretaker. Any other explanation would have made it incredibly uncomfortable to continue to invest in Blackburn and Mills Construction Development, or to attend Rachel's and Chow's Easter Party – truly an amazing fête by any standards.

★

"I think Chow is going to regret getting involved with that lot. Once you get into the mud with them, that's that." Kathy, like Jackie, was surprised and titillated by Chow's decision.

"Can you imagine Rachel and the President's wife having lunch?" Jackie's comment made them all laugh, especially Kathy.

"No, wait, what about dinner? It serves Missy right." Jackie enjoyed another jab at Rachel.

"You can take the girl out of the country but you can't take the country out of the girl." This time only Mrs. B laughed at Kathy's comment. Jackie's mother had come from the country, so she didn't enjoy this last knock at the President's wife, known to many as the Empress, who was mocked for her garish, unpolished ways. Those in Mrs. B's circle who had been invited to the President's house claimed the Empress could barely manage a knife, a fork and a sentence all at once. At one time there was a photograph, from an anonymous source of course, posted on the Internet, of the Empress dressed in a gold and silver gown, eating her rice and peas with a spoon. She seldom spoke at functions and that, according to Kathy, was to her benefit; when she did, local, regional and foreign dignitaries would be forced to hide their smiles as verbs and subjects disagreed, pronouns could never find the right nouns, adjectives switched places with adverbs and her accent fell somewhere in between Toronto and Tobago. The Empress never failed to amuse many in Mrs. B's world. A minority, Ruthie and Claire among them, pitied her, for she was not dangerous, as was her husband, just uneducated, and uncultured in the ways of the paler Northerners on the island.

Mrs. B had come to their monthly lunch with a purpose. She had to let Kathy and Jackie know about her visit to Martinique, had to make it sound natural so that Kathy would not start one of her often delicious rumours.

Mrs. B waited for a natural pause in the conversation, after they had crushed the Empress, impaled Chow, chewed over Rachel yet again, and thoroughly analysed one of the most uneventful Carnivals on record (apart from a stabbing when a fight broke out between two security guards). Only then did Mrs. B say that she was going to Martinique on a little vacation.

"Another honeymoon?" Kathy looked meaningfully at Jackie.

"No, Charles isn't going this time, just me on my lonesome…"

"Charles doesn't mind you running off for two weeks?" Jackie could not imagine leaving Sparky for that long, even though he had left her for the last Two World Cups and was currently considering going to South Africa on yet another "Boys' Lime".

"Charles was fine with it when I told him. I guess he thinks I need the rest. It's not been that easy with Ruthie. You know what I mean…"

"Of course, I know it hasn't been easy. How is she doing now anyway?" Kathy had seen Ruthie and Monique on the beach a couple of Sundays ago. "She still spends a lot of time with that girl." Kathy wanted to say "little slut" but she held back.

"Ruthie's okay. She seems to be getting back on her feet. In the last few weeks she's been in a better mood. And as for her friendship with that one, I can't really do too much. At least she has someone to talk too." Mrs. B had softened her position on Monique, especially since the rumour about her affair with Chow turned out to be false, although Kathy assured them that the one with "the Arab" as she called him, was fact not fiction. Mrs. B told her friends about Diamant, the rock in the sea and the room she had booked with a view of it. Kathy and Jackie agreed that all married woman their age needed to take a break once in a while, just to recharge and recuperate. Jackie said it was good for any marriage and Kathy agreed, although neither of them had ever left their husbands.

It would be their last lunch until Mrs. B came back, Jackie noted when they hugged and kissed in the car park. Mrs. B said that she would call them before she left, even though she knew she wouldn't. She just wanted to leave without providing any more details. As Mrs. B drove away, Kathy and Jackie waved as though they were already at the airport sending her off on her solo adventure.

"Something is going on. Why would she just pick up and go to Martinique? Lena never does stuff like that," Kathy said.

They chatted in the parking lot for quite a while discussing their friend and her many problems. There was obviously trouble in paradise. Charles and "poor" Elena had to be having problems for her to want to go away without him. It had to be Ruthie. Ruthie was breaking up the marriage; Ruthie was the root of all evil in the household. It wouldn't be long before some other Ruthie disaster would bring the whole structure down. Their friend was putting up a good front but they knew better; her marriage was falling apart. Kathy would repeat this to mutual friends (swearing them to secrecy) whenever there was a lull in the conversation or Kathy wanted to make her presence felt in the room. Mrs. B would have been distressed to learn how little of what she'd said had been heard. Kathy told quite a few people that Marie Elena had gone to St. Martin, and when other friends corrected her, she said location was just a detail, the reason why was more important.

★

Mrs. B had lied to her friends about Charles's reaction; he did not like the fact that she was going away without him. He was not okay with it at all. It had been a long time since Charles had reacted in such a demonstrative way – which pleased Mrs. B. Indeed, his response – asking her why she was leaving and if she was going alone – aroused her like some heady aphrodisiac and so they made love that very night, even though, or perhaps because, they had argued all day. The next morning Charles thought that their lovemaking meant that she had changed her mind and was going to cancel her trip. When she informed him that she had no intention of doing this, Charles retreated to his default mode. He told her she could do what the hell she liked and went to the office without finishing the French toast he had made especially for her. That night they barely spoke to each other and Mrs. B slept in Ruthie's old room.

★

Ruthie couldn't believe her luck; her mother would be away for the Professor's five-day visit, which fell smack in the middle of the Martinique trip.

"You deserve a break, Mummy. We have been through so much these last few months."

"Well, you'll have to take care of your father. He's not used to my not being around. I've arranged for Milly to come every day and half-day on Saturday."

"She doesn't have to come on Saturday, we'll be fine. We can always buy rotis or Chinese food. Really, don't make poor Milly travel all that way just for us."

Mrs. B said that she had already taken care of it and that all Ruthie had to do was to make sure that someone was there to open up for Milly. The enthusiasm Ruthie expressed for her trip was almost disturbing.

With only a few days to go before Mrs. B's departure and the Professor's arrival, the San Pedro townhouse seemed abuzz with activity. Both his wife and daughter were moving around as though they had found gold in some hidden trove but had forgotten to tell Charles where it was. He sat by and watched as though he was in the audience of a film featuring his wife and daughter. Then more arresting news came through on all the government-owned radio stations. At midday it was announced that the youngest, most dynamic member of the opposition party, Mark Singh, had committed suicide, hanging himself after he had shot his wife and his two sons in the head while they were asleep. There had been a rumour going around that Singh had been plotting to overthrow the leader of the opposition party who, as the nation knew, had no intention of putting up a fight against the President and his election army. The police said they found cocaine hidden in a safe where Singh had also kept his gun. But that was not all; two days later, Singh's partner in his law firm also died when his brakes gave way driving home one night. The police found cocaine in his car as well.

No one dared say that the coincidence was astounding, that Singh had been happily married for five years and had no reason to kill himself or his family; nor that Simon Conrad had ever been known for reckless driving, heavy drinking or dabbling in cocaine. But that was the story that the newspapers put out, and the President wrote a long letter to the editor offering his condolences, but warning the youth of the nation about the dangers of drug addiction.

No one tried to uncover what Singh and Conrad had discovered about the President. But the rumour was that photographs had been sent to Singh showing the President and two Colombian drug lords having dinner at the President's residence, and that Singh also had a short video filmed on a phone of the President embracing the two men while the Empress stood by with a vacant expression on her face. The story went that Singh and Conrad had sent everything to an editor they trusted at one of the newspapers but nothing was published. Every member of the President's Cabinet attended the funeral wearing a dark suit and a sad face. The President himself wiped away a tear and the Empress sobbed as if it were her two sons lying in the small coffins at the front of the church. Mrs. B saw the broadcast as she was packing for Martinique.

# CHAPTER FOUR
## TRANSLATIONS

The Professor did not look like the Professor; he had shrunk. Ruthie heard a voice she recognized but saw an unrecognizable figure coming towards her as she lay on her favourite deckchair at the hotel pool. She had oiled her tanned body, slicked back her hair in a Jennifer Lopez twist, even put on a little make-up. On her drive to the hotel, she'd felt the butterflies, the headiness, the desire – everything had returned as though she were about to meet him once again in the apartment on that shady Cambridge street. But there was a thin, pinkish-white body in black Speedos and a white tee-shirt approaching her; his once thick brown hair had been buzz-cut too close to the skull in an obvious attempt to hide the onset of balding; his face was half-hidden behind oversized frames – too big for a man; his pink hands held a soft cloth bag with newspapers and perhaps a book. Ruthie could never have imagined feeling such repulsion towards this grinning stranger, claiming to be her Professor, about to bend over and give her a wet kiss on the cheek. She accepted his compliments graciously. He said she looked absolutely amazing. She lied and told him similar nice things, how glad she was to see him, and could at last show him her home. She asked about the conference in Cuba; he told her all about Havana, because the conference itself had been a waste of time. The invited writer, Martinez, and the specialist on Martinez, J.R. Barrows had both cancelled at the last minute (there was talk that they might have actually planned the sabotage since neither had received the promised advance from the organizers). But Havana, the Professor said, was an experience that had actually outdone the one he had in Haiti a few years ago.

Ruthie listened as he droned on. The Professor always talked in paragraphs that soon became full-blown essays with cross references, footnotes and anecdotes (for light relief) until he returned to the main theme – Havana. But even though the Professor's ideas were like brilliant sparks, and his descriptions of the landscape poetic, Ruthie kept thinking how badly he translated in her home. Translated was the only word that came to mind. She compared her Boston Professor to the Professor here. In Boston he read well, blending in, yet still able to stand out; no one in Harvard Square would have questioned his intelligent good looks, and quick wit. But here in Trinidad, he just looked like a skinny, white, probably gay tourist dressing a little too young for his age. She couldn't imagine taking him outside the hotel (the only place where he didn't really stand out), nor introducing him to Monique, who had never actually seen a picture of the Professor. Ruthie wondered if *she* had not translated well in Boston. What had she looked like to the Professor? Was he equally embarrassed to introduce her to his world? But then he didn't have to; mistresses do not have to be introduced; the arrangement suited him perfectly.

It was nearly eleven o'clock by the time the Professor had finished telling her about Havana. Although he asked her more than once, Ruthie said very little about what she had done in the past ten months (really, not very much), and of course neither of them brought up the miscarriage.

"This is where I have spent most of the time, or walking around the Savannah. I'll take you there, just down the hill, not far. I didn't, no I haven't looked for a job… It's hard when you come back."

"Yes, it must take time and then you had a lot on your plate." By plate the Professor meant the pregnancy.

"But at least I've finally become a good reader, managed to read all the books I never finished for my courses and I even read some of the ones you recommended. They seem to make more sense now, outside the classroom."

She told him that she had just ordered Martinez's latest, but in translation since she no longer had any faith in her Spanish. *The Writer* should arrive next week. The Professor said he had read it and it was definitely Martinez's weakest, and unbearably self-indulgent, even for Martinez. "Masturbation on the page," was the way the Professor described it and Ruthie wasn't quite sure whether he meant it or simply wanted to introduce a sexual theme into their conversation. Her Professor was always horny.

The bad translation made Ruthie rapidly rewrite the script of the romantic movie she had imagined. She needed a little time to get used to the way the Professor looked to her now. She needed to acclimatize herself to the situation, to this Professor in this location. They ate lunch together, the Professor ordering a chicken roti, even though Ruthie warned him that hotels were not where one ordered roti, but he didn't listen (he had heard so much about "the local delicacy"). She ordered a hamburger and fries, much to his dismay, saying that she had become too Americanized. She knew such food was the best the poolside restaurant could offer and promised to take him to a proper roti shop the next day. After the meal and a couple of cold beers, she could tell that the Professor wanted her to come up to his room, but even with a slight buzz from the beers, Ruthie did not feel any desire to make love to him. She needed more time or more beers, even though a hot hook-up on the first day had been part of her original plan. In fact, she had seen herself spending the entire afternoon in her Professor's room, making up for lost time. Ruthie had to lie. She said she had to get back home to check on the housekeeper; with her mother in Martinique and her father at work, she had to lock up after Milly. She promised to come back later that afternoon so they could have dinner. The Professor let her know that he was disappointed, but said he would have dinner sent up to his room that evening so they could spend some time together – which Ruthie knew translated as sex. Before she left he handed her two gifts from his bag, a beautiful book on contemporary Cuban artists and a CD of a singer that Ruthie used to listen to while she was in Boston. These gifts, coupled with the lies she had told, left Ruthie feeling a little ashamed, as she drove away from the hotel in her mother's car.

★

From the moment she walked into her hotel room on the second floor and opened the sliding door, Mrs. B felt as though a great burden had been lifted. She had a clear view of the large rock, Le Diamant, in the calm sea. It was low season now and except for a few high-pitched shrieks coming from metropolitan and Martinican children in the pool below, the hotel was quiet, almost still. For the next couple of hours Mrs. B unpacked, nibbled on some nuts she had bought in the airport in St Lucia and then sat on the verandah facing the Diamant rock. It was only around two in the afternoon, when she began to feel extremely hungry with a *faim de loup,* that she decided to shower and dress for her first Martinican meal.

Mrs. B's French was rusty but she was determined to get by. It had been a while since she had attacked those "r"s and she tried to make her heavy Trinidadian tongue a little lighter. Her mother and all of her aunts spoke and wrote beautiful French, but Mrs. B had never been one for languages. It drove Simone crazy when the French cousins visited to practice their English, but Marie-Elena refused to practice her French. The memory still haunted her of the times when her mother would ask her questions in French and she could barely reply or would say some word or phrase that caused the entire table of relatives to burst into hysterical laughter, a real *fourire.* But now without an audience or Simone's judgments, Mrs. B felt liberated; she would try to speak for the next two weeks mocked or not. Fortunately, the hotel staff at *Les Caraïbes* spoke some English and were kind to her.

Diamant was a small quaint town; pretty, clean and tasteful like many others along this side of the island. Charles's Martinican relatives, the Valmonts, had a beach house on a hill overlooking the bay. But even though there were people she knew on both sides of the family, she had no intention of calling on them. She wanted to control her time and not be forced into lunches, drinks and tiring translations between French and English – although truth be told, their English was a billion times better than her French. She remembered, too, the Valmont family reunions she and Charles had attended, how when the ritual of family cheers, chants and toasts became too much to bear, she and Charles would slip away to a bar-restaurant called Yvonne's. Would it still be there?

Mrs. B set off through the town, past the bakery, the handsome white church, the town hall, the boutiques, the pharmacy, and headed towards where she remembered Yvonne's had been. She passed a family of four – mother, father, son and daughter – dressed for the beach carrying baskets, baguettes and bottled water – French, no doubt, looking like something out of a magazine.

When she first stepped out of the hotel, she'd felt uneasy, foreign and alone, but the more she walked towards the centre of the town the calmer she grew. The *bonjours* she passed were always pleasant, but dining alone was not something that she did at home. There she would always see someone she knew who would invite her to join their party, with a look of some pity. Here, though, she felt the freedom of anonymity.

The actual name of Yvonne's restaurant was *Le Raisin de Mer* but no one called it by that name. Yvonne was renowned both for her beauty and her famous *accras* – both had been featured in tourists magazines in the US and Europe. Even before Mrs. B walked into the restaurant, she could smell Yvonne's *accras*.

The décor was simple and tasteful. There was a room with wooden tables and bar, and a second dining area outside, where chairs and tables were arranged on the sand around the sea grape trees. Mrs. B was a little disappointed to be greeted by a young, white waitress with a very Parisian accent; Yvonne was absent. Mrs. B used phrases like *l'autre salle* and *près de la mer* even *en plein air*. The girl warned Mrs. B about the *chaleur*, but led her outside. Mrs. B sat under one of the trees and ordered a Lorraine, the beer the locals drank, a tamarind juice and a plate of *accras*. Although she had brought a book with her, Sue Miller's *The Senator's Wife*, which Ruthie had given to her, Mrs. B didn't open it. She ate her *accras* and watched the activities of the French family she had seen on the road. They had set up camp a little further down the beach. Mrs. B noted the mother's – she looked late thirties – neatly tanned French body and even neater French breasts and her slender, tall, blond husband in his Speedos.

By the time the waitress came back with her second course of *steak hâché* and *frites* (not exactly what Mrs. B wanted, but it was the easiest item to pronounce), she felt as though she could sit under that tree and stare at the family for the next ten years of her life. She enjoyed, too, the guilty pleasure of such an unsophisticated meal when Yvonne's menu had so much more to offer. Then she heard laughter coming from the room inside and the spectacular Yvonne appeared at her table. The waitress must have spoken to her because Yvonne greeted her in English. Mrs. B would have liked to pretend she was Martinican just a little longer.

Yvonne looked stunning in a white *broderie anglaise* dress that fell just below her knees and a white headdress. Mrs. B couldn't help but notice all the yellow gold around her neck, wrists, and the huge gold hoops in her ears. The Antilleans had style and Yvonne more than most.

"Your family is here with you?" Yvonne's question puzzled Mrs. B. She wasn't sure whether Yvonne had actually recognized her or was just making polite conversation.

"No, they're at home."

"And where is home?"

"Trinidad is home," Mrs. B said, with an emphasis that surprised her. "I have family here, too, the Valmonts, but I don't keep in touch with them."

"Family is important, you don't think?" Yvonne said with a wide smile.

"Depends on the family," Mrs. B said.

Yvonne laughed like a young girl being tickled.

But before Yvonne could question her further, Mrs. B changed the topic, asking about when the market opened on Saturday and the best way to visit Mont Pelée. She had done this once before with Charles when Ruthie was still a baby and she wanted to visit the site again. Before Mrs. B left the restaurant, Yvonne told her about the boutique she owned, and Mrs. B promised to visit it and said that she would probably be back for lunch the following day, unless she went into Fort de France.

"It's not so pretty now you know. All the *toxicomanes* from Paris, the *drogues*, they all come here now."

Mrs. B explained that she wanted to buy some madras material to make a tablecloth and napkins, and Yvonne assured her that she had madras in the boutique, including the same pattern she used on the restaurant tablecloths and that she should look there first.

★

When Monique got Ruthie's text message asking her to come to

San Pedro immediately, she imagined the worst, that the Professor had hurt Ruthie again. So when she arrived at the house and Ruthie started to talk about bad translation and the way the Professor's shades made him look gay, Monique was relieved, then amused. Miss Boston was no longer attracted to her pink Professor. Indeed, the idea of making love to him was bordering on repulsive.

"Maybe if he got a tan and put on some surfer shorts, he might look better."

Monique was smiling, but for Ruthie this was no joke. She wanted the Professor to disappear, as if in a magic trick, because the magic was gone.

"What am I supposed to do for the next five days?"

"Get sick. Say you have some STD – that usually works; or say your father is sick and you have to stay with him."

"I don't want to put goat mouth on my father."

"Well he doesn't know where you live, right? You could just not answer your cell, texts, or emails for the next few days."

"You mean lie low, that sort of thing… No, seriously, Monique. I don't understand it, maybe I'm just still very angry…"

"Yeah, maybe it's not just how he looks. Maybe you just don't feel anything for him any more. Maybe it's not just the sexy little black Speedos…"

"Why did I say yes to him coming here?" Ruthie went into the kitchen and brought out a bottle of her mother's best wine.

"Guess he just doesn't have that power over you any more."

"And that can't be a bad thing?"

"No, idiot, it means you're free. Free to enjoy your life, do what you want. Forget him."

When the Professor called Ruthie later that evening she lied again. She was not feeling well; she had a migraine and a slight fever. She promised to come over in the morning, once she felt better. As she expected, the Professor sounded irritated; he wanted to make Ruthie feel guilty, to make her feel responsible for bringing him all this way only to be left on his own. When his complaints were met with silence, he changed his tone, offered to pick her up in a taxi, saying he had a special home remedy for headaches. But nothing worked for the Professor the way it used to and before Ruthie could say sorry he put down the phone, took a shower and dressed for dinner in the hotel dining room. Later that night he called Ruthie on her cell phone but she let it go to voicemail.

★

Mrs. B hadn't slept well after her call home and a brief, tense conversation with Charles, who still seemed angry. Ruthie wasn't unfriendly, but she too sounded as though something was bothering her. During the night, Mrs. B had concluded that the trip was a bad idea and that she wouldn't stay for the whole two weeks. However, by morning, after coffee and croissants on her small verandah, she felt purposeful again.

With nobody much to talk to, the morning passed slowly. Mrs. B told herself she was enjoying the solitude, but she got dressed and set out for Yvonne's as soon as it opened its doors. This time she was more adventurous with her order: a Lorraine, a plate of *accras*, and Creole fish with rice and salad. She watched a group of couples, probably from France, who lay on the beach tanning, chatting and smoking. There was no sign of the family and no sign of Yvonne. But just as Mrs. B had resigned herself to that fact, Yvonne made her grand entrance and approached Mrs. B's table with a warm *"Bon après-midi"*. Yvonne was in her usual white – this time palazzo pants and a white tank top. Her dark brown curly hair brushed her shoulders in a wild way that Mrs. B thought looked gloriously wonderful in Martinique but would definitely appear a little crazy at home.

*"Tu as bien dormi?"*

Mrs. B felt flattered to be spoken to in French, though the most she could muster was a *"très bien"* and an *"et toi?"* She had yet to visit Yvonne's boutique and she felt the need to say this, promising to go immediately after lunch. Unfortunately, her French betrayed her here; Yvonne replied in English, saying she could go at any time.

"Have you ever visited Haiti? You know that's where my husband's from." Yvonne was now sitting at Mrs. B's table.

Mrs. B said no, but she had always wanted to, and asked, "What is it like?"

"I don't know, my *mari* says it is at once beautiful and ugly."

121

"So you've never visited Haiti?"

"*Non, jamais,* my husband is Haitian but I have not been to Haiti. Actually, he lives in New York now, since three years, before that he lived in Miami. I lived in New York with him for a while. I still visit every year in August."

Mrs. B was confused. Again her French and her manners held her back. She thought Yvonne had said that she had family in Haiti. She was curious about these bizarre marriage arrangements. But *politesse* prevailed so she ventured, "Il fait beau aujourd'hui."

But Yvonne went back to the subject. "We are not really married, you know, although he is like my husband."

Mrs. B nodded her head in agreement, though she didn't quite get the "not really". In Mrs. B's world, you were either wife or mistress, ex-wife or ex-mistress.

"He is a writer you know, my *mari*."

"Really, what's his name?"

"Henri Laguerre."

"*La guerre* is war isn't it?"

"That's right, but it does not describe him." Yvonne said. Mrs. B was happy to have understood this. "He is a very tranquil, gentle man with no enemies, not crazy and jealous like me." At least that was how Mrs. B translated Yvonne's words.

"What does he write about?"

"He writes about Haitians living in New York, but now he is working on a book about the earthquake. He lost a brother and an uncle. It was so terrible."

They spoke about the earthquake for a while and then Yvonne moved on to greet another table of tourists from Bordeaux.

Mrs. B hired a private taxi that afternoon and drove to Mont Pelée to explore the site of another earthquake, more than a century earlier than the one in Haiti. Her driver Max waited while she walked around the town and visited the small museum devoted to the tragedy. Max also drove her to a black sand beach where she took a quick dip. The water was a dark emerald colour and the sand stuck to her feet like tar. Although Max's English was not as good as Yvonne's, it was better than Mrs. B's French, so they managed to get by. He was not overly talkative,

122

spoke at the right time and left Mrs. B to wander around her own thoughts as they drove over the mountains. He told her about "an adorable café" in the town of Trois Islets where she had a deliciously cold pomme-de-cythère juice and a guava tart. She had brought her Sue Miller book with her, mainly for protection from unwanted conversations and fresh young men, but she didn't need it. No one bothered her, and this made Mrs. B feel old and a little sad.

★

Ruthie had finally found the courage to tell her Professor, by phone, that she was terribly sorry and that it had been a mistake to have him come to Trinidad. The Professor did not take the news well. He had put his marriage in jeopardy by coming, and he called Ruthie all the nasty names that came into his head, and there were many. When Ruthie put the phone down, he called back, begging Ruthie to come back to Boston with him. He even hinted at leaving his wife.

"What would I be going back to?"

"We could be together," he said.

"We were together before and it was a mess. I was a mess."

"You're not happy here, Ruthie. It's obvious. You have no life. Wasting time at a hotel pool, that's what you've come back to."

"No, you're right, I'm not happy, but I wasn't happy in Boston either."

"Well you certainly put on a good show; I can recall a lot of happiness in the Cambridge apartment."

"And what about the clinic? That was happiness?"

"I need to see you. We need to discuss all of this, we need to say everything, get it all out. It's not really possible on the phone."

"I know why you want to see me and it's not to discuss anything."

"Okay, I miss you, all of you. It takes nothing for me to admit it, and I want you to come back."

The conversation went around like this for a while and Ruthie even enjoyed the flirting and the way she had the Professor pursuing her. But this time she was setting the rules and he couldn't get into her head as in the old days. As soon as the Professor realized that there was to be no goodbye fuck, he wished Ruthie the best, apologized for the vulgarity of the first call and hung up. He left the hotel that same afternoon and spent the next few days in Tobago, where he met a beautiful Tobagonian beach girl and spent the next two days mostly in his hotel room having as much sex as he could manage. She was not expensive, especially when he converted her price to US dollars.

Ruthie, who had spent so many months at the hotel poolside, now no longer felt like going back there; maybe the Professor had spoiled it for her, or maybe, as Monique said, he had released her from the prison she had made for herself since she lost Maria. Ruthie could not explain it to herself, and she didn't try to. In a few months, her year's membership would be up and she had no intention of renewing it. But she had to find something to do to fill her day, so she offered to help her father in his office. His evident joy at that offer took her aback, and she realized that she had made him happier than she had intended. She knew he had always hoped she would become interested in the family business, but she wasn't planning to spend more time there than necessary – until she found a job that she really liked. But he looked so lost since her mother left for Martinique that she didn't want to spoil his good mood by saying this.

The next day she found herself sitting next to one of the secretaries being given a quick course on the filing systems and the client database. Charles kept popping his head in and out of the office, sometimes for a real reason but mostly just to smile at the sight of his daughter. They had lunch together and talked in a relaxed, light way that would have been impossible had her mother been present.

★

Mrs. B spent Sunday, her last full day, at the popular beach of Salines. Yvonne had offered to take her there along with the waitress, Marianne, and the bartender, Louis-Philippe. Sunday was the day for the locals but they managed to get a parking spot close to the large restaurant tents where they would have lunch. As soon as Yvonne and Marianne had spread the beach towels they both took off their bikini tops. Mrs. B had no intention of baring her breasts, but felt self-conscious in her one-piece bathing suit. Yvonne's breasts were heavier than Marianne's but she looked just as relaxed. Mrs. B envied her, knowing that she could never feel such freedom in her body.

As Marianne covered him in sun block, Louis-Philippe made a joke in Creole that Mrs. B didn't understand. Yvonne exploded with a laugh that her Aunt Claire would have described as a market woman cackle. It must have been a very crude joke because Yvonne didn't translate for Mrs. B, who suspected that the joke was about Marianne, but she didn't seem to understand the Creole either, but laughed anyway. It soon became obvious that Marianne and Louis-Philippe, who headed for the sea, were lovers.

"I have lost a lot of waitresses because of Louis-Philippe," Yvonne said, as though it was an inevitable outcome. "He is not beautiful but he has charm and that is very dangerous. Marianne is too innocent for him."

Innocent was not the first word that popped into Mrs. B's head when she saw Marianne snaked around Louis-Philippe in the sea, but perhaps "innocent" translated differently here. Perhaps it had nothing to do with sex and more with innocent expectations – those that Marianne may have had about herself and Louis-Philippe.

"My daughter is like that, I think, too trusting of others." Mrs. B had no idea why she said this but she felt compelled to say something. She had never thought of Ruthie as innocent or trusting but she realized that in this place, with people who knew nothing about her past or even her present, she could create an interesting character for herself and for anyone close to her. She could say anything and whether they chose to believe her or not didn't really matter.

"Do you trust like your daughter?"

"No, we're very different; I find it very difficult to trust anyone."

"I know. It's hard to even trust you, I mean yourself sometimes." Yvonne smiled wryly.

"I think I trust happiness least of all." Mrs. B was not lying this time. Whenever she felt too happy, she became uneasy, aware of how fleeting the feeling would be. She could only wait for it to disappear.

"Why do you have to trust it?"

Mrs. B just smiled and wished that she had never brought up

the idea of trust; these were matters that she did not want to discuss with a stranger, even one as friendly as Yvonne.

"My Henri was supposed to be visiting me this week but he has to work."

"I thought you said he was a writer."

"Yes, of course he is a writer, but he still has to have a job. He cannot eat off his writing."

Mrs. B did not correct Yvonne to say "live off" instead of "eat" because she sensed that she had irritated Yvonne in some way. She tried to undo the damage by asking what Henri's job was.

"He is a carpenter; he is very good."

"I'm sure he is," Mrs. B said.

Yvonne did not seem herself, at least she was not the self that Mrs. B had become used to seeing. She assumed that the mood had to do with Henri's absence. Mrs. B reflected that she had not really thought about Charles in days.

"You never talk about your home," Yvonne said. "Do you miss your family?"

"Yes, very much."

"Sometimes it's good to escape." Yvonne may have meant "get away" but somehow escape better described what Mrs. B felt she had tried to do.

"Yes, I guess so."

"I am thinking to join Henri in New York, I miss him too much." Yvonne lit another cigarette. They had just finished eating their lunch under one of the tents and the owner, Achille, whom Yvonne evidently knew well, came over to say hello.

They stayed at Achille's for most of the day drinking Lorraines and moving in and out of French, Creole and English. Catherine (Achille's girlfriend), Louis-Philippe and Marianne eventually joined them. They spoke about love, sex with a stranger, marriage, children (none of them had children except Mrs. B; Catherine did not want to have a baby; Achille seemed to be longing for one). They tried to speak as much English as they could for Mrs. B's benefit and when she didn't understand, Yvonne, whose sad mood had lifted, would translate. They did not leave the beach before sunset and Mrs. B felt that it had been her best day in Martinique, and one of the happiest days she had spent in a long time.

# CHAPTER FIVE
## GIFTS

Mrs. B didn't know what gift to get for Charles, but there had to be something; she felt quite guilty over enjoying herself so much – almost as much as over her affair with Larry. Simone used to say it was all Eve's fault, that guilt from the apple had become a woman's cancer.

Choosing Ruthie's gift was easy; Mrs. B bought her daughter a book by the famous Martinican poet Aimé Césaire, who had just died. She didn't know whether Ruthie already had his work, but was sure that she wouldn't have this new edition, which included photographs of the poet with the famous writers and politicians he knew. But Charles was not a reader like Ruthie; in the end she bought a coffee-table book about yachting and races around the French Caribbean isles; it had beautiful photographs and only a small amount of text in French. However, from the moment she walked out of the Librairie des Caraïbes in Fort de France she realized it was a mistake. At the airport she was persuaded to buy the latest cologne from Chanel for her *mari*. The citrus base was light and refreshing, but on the plane she sniffed it again; it was also a mistake; Charles seldom wore cologne. By the last leg of the plane trip to Trinidad she was panicking; she thought about buying Charles an expensive watch at the airport, but she was sure that he would never take off the one he had inherited from his father. After looking at three Mont Blanc pens, she decided to get him wine. She should have bought the wine in Martinique, but the limited selection in the Trinidad duty free would have to do. Armed with book, cologne and wine she felt less apprehensive and guilty about the reunion. But Mrs. B would soon learn that she was mistaken in thinking that she had to appease an angry husband. Charles had long gotten over his wife's solo vacation. Every angry thought had been supplanted by the joy and pride he felt at being able to tell his mother, brother and any friend he met on the street that his one and only Ruthie was working with him. So instead of meeting a sour face at the airport, Mrs. B found a smiling husband. He kissed her on both cheeks, asked about her trip, took her hand luggage and left her feeling relieved but confused.

As she waited for Charles to bring the car, there was a sudden commotion. Three police outriders and three black Prados pulled up to the Departure area. Emerging from the middle vehicle was Larry and the Minister of Trade. They were surrounded by bodyguards and minions in ill-fitting suits with cell phones attached to their ears. Larry stood out, looking very white and impeccably tailored. She heard his laugh as he shared a joke with the minister, tapping his shoulder like an old friend. She saw the minister and Larry enter the doors of the airport after the bodyguards had cleared the way. She wasn't sure if Larry saw her and made no move to wave to him.

When Charles returned she described what she had witnessed.

"Yeah, since the elections announcement, Chow in the papers every day, always skinning and grinning with one of those jokers." The pace of campaigning had picked up and the President was being seen in areas that he had not visited during the last five years. Chow had become an important symbol of the new party image. The President wanted to show that the local white and high brown business classes were ready to give open support to the party. Charles had saved all the newspaper articles featuring Chow, including an extensive interview entitled "Family First, Business Second". They both laughed at the title but for different reasons. As they left the airport, Mrs. B noticed the gigantic billboard of the President smiling benignly, with the caption: "Thank You Mr. President. You are a Gift to the Nation."

On the way home, Charles couldn't wait to give his wife the news about Ruthie. She was managing really well, learning all the office skills so quickly, and getting along with the secretaries. Mrs. B knew that it was something Charles had always wanted. His brother Robby had his sons in line to take over their share of the business and now Charles had Ruthie. He described their morning's together, doubles from Captain, lunch at the corner roti shop. Charles spoke as if Ruthie had been working there for months rather than a week. He barely asked Mrs. B about Martinique.

Mrs. B was sure that Ruthie wouldn't last in the office; she had never shown any interest before, but she didn't want to spoil it for Charles so she played along. When they got to the compound, the security guards were patrolling with more pit bulls and guns than usual. They stopped Charles as he was about to turn into the driveway.

"Evening, Mr. Butcher. We had a prowler, so we asking residents to stay inside 'til we sweep the compound."

Charles parked and rushed inside to check on Ruthie; the note on the fridge said she had gone to the movies with Monique.

"Ruthie's gone out. She should know better. Election time is not a good time to lime late."

"But it's not late, Charles. She'll be fine."

Charles didn't listen to his wife. He called Ruthie on her cell. She didn't reply, so he left a message saying that there was a prowler on the property and that she should be careful coming in. Only then did he realize that his wife had gone out to bring her suitcases from the car. Mrs. B went to the kitchen to see Ruthie's empty glass on the counter and a half-eaten plate of Milly's pelau in the sink. Couldn't the girl have waited to see her instead of going to the movies? Mrs. B didn't unpack that night. She ate, showered, then went to bed. Charles claimed he wasn't tired but she knew that he was downstairs, waiting for Ruthie to come home. The next morning Mrs. B woke up to an empty house. Charles and Ruthie had left for work and she had a day of nothing planned ahead of her.

★

Ruthie couldn't tell her mother that she had already read *Cahier d'un retour au pays natal* at least twice for a literature paper; her mother seemed so proud when she handed it to her, she could only say thanks. The *Cahier* was on her desk when Chow walked into the office followed by the bodyguard assigned to him. Ruthie had never liked Chow, or Rachel, or their incredibly stuck-up children. Ruthie had heard Chow make horrible racist remarks about coolies and niggers when he felt comfortable with his close friends, which unfortunately included her parents. When she pointed this out to her father, he told her that Chow was just joking, and that she was getting on like one of those politically correct Americans. But Ruthie knew what a joke sounded like. To think that Chow was now with the same coolies and niggers he despised – Ruthie didn't think she could dislike him any more than she already did.

Chow gave her a light kiss on the cheek and stood next to her desk. "How you going, Miss Butcher? Enjoying your father's boring work?" Chow always found a way to put down her father.

"Better than being a boring housewife."

"I hope your mother doesn't hear you calling her boring," Chow said laughing.

Ruthie wanted to say I meant your boring ass wife, but just then her father came out, apologizing to Chow for keeping him waiting.

"No problem, Ruthie was keeping me company." Chow winked at her.

Chow didn't sit when Charles offered him a seat; he said he was in a hurry to get back to the office.

"Listen, I came to invite you and Elena to a party at the house."

"You came all the way here to say that? You could have called."

"Well I wanted to prepare you for the guests. We not having the usual suspects; we mixing the old with the new. Some people from the party will be there and they want to talk to my friends about some things."

"You couldn't be asking me to party with those people? My only experience of doing business with them meant not getting paid for three years after we finished the job."

"Listen, Charlie boy, you know and I know what the result is going to be, so there's no sense fighting the inevitable. Is like boxing with a ghost."

"I not doing any business with ghosts, but thanks for the invite."

Chow laughed but repeated that all the "boys" were coming and they were on board to talk business.

Charles stayed behind his desk, not walking Chow out. He wished he could talk to his father, but had to make do with Robby.

"Yes, me too. Chow passed by my office yesterday to talk about some party. The finance boy, Sammy, want to discuss something, some project. You going or not?"

"You can't be serious, a project with those people?"

"Which people in particular? Those on our side or theirs?"

"Robby, this is no joke."

"I'm not joking, Charles."

"Robby we did things with them before. You forget what happen or what?"

"Listen Charlie, your best man, best partner is the one who invite me."

"Right, you do what you want, Robby. Any financing better not come from the business."

"You mean my half of the business?"

Charles did not want to have this fight, so he just cut off and ended the conversation. It had not been a good day; a foreign client was complaining about an insurance policy claim on a yacht that had gotten damaged while they were working on it (Robby had neglected to tell Charles about the incident), and two of the secretaries had called in sick.

★

At lunch, sitting across from each other on the verandah of an old colonial house that had been converted into a restaurant, Ruthie could see that her father was upset. It had to be because of Chow's visit. She wouldn't usually pry, but these days she felt emboldened to ask, "What happened with Chow?"

"Nothing," her father said, but then changed his tone. "He wants me to give money to the party."

"That's so frigging disgusting, Daddy." Ruthie had suspected that Chow's visit had something to do with the elections; he was all over the newspaper laughing it up with the President and his cronies.

"It's not frigging disgusting, Ruthie. It's just politics."

"Exactly, same thing. He knows how you feel; and what about all the things he used to say about them?"

"Chow is a businessman, sweetie, and now he's a politician as well."

Ruthie didn't want to go too far. She could see the disappointment and confusion in her father's face. They kept off the subject of Chow for the rest of the meal, and Ruthie avoided talking about her intention to stop working at the office very soon.

★

Mrs. B was giving Milly instructions about the chicken marsala for lunch when the phone rang. It was Aunt Claire. After a few polite exchanges Claire came to the purpose of her call.

"I need to talk to you about Simone; she's not doing very well these days."

"Not doing very well in what way?"

"Michael says she refuses to eat or leave the house. She just stays in bed staring at the TV; he thinks it's worse this time."

Mrs. B knew that these dark moods were part of her family history. There had been an aunt who had committed suicide while away at boarding school in England, and a brilliant young uncle who killed himself soon after he started his degree at Yale. There was, of course, the episode with Ruthie in Boston. Still, Mrs. B had not associated these dark moods with her mother. If anything, Simone seemed manic about living her life to the full, to the point of selfishness.

It was Christmas when Mrs. B had last seen her parents, when the Roumain family had Christmas lunch together. Mrs. B could recall nothing particularly strange about her mother then. Ruthie had not been in a good mood, but she was seldom in a good mood during such family gatherings and the pregnancy had made it worse. She did not want to be on display and had managed to hide from the rest of the family for most of the time. She had gained a lot of weight, said she felt like a whale, ready to be harpooned by the likes of her grandmother Simone. Ruthie was not disappointed; it took Simone less than two minutes to say that in her day women only gained twelve pounds, while Ruthie was closer to forty at that point, and still had a few months to go. Mrs. B, in turn, had been offended by Simone's comment about how gaunt she looked, how at fifty (Mrs. B didn't like to remind her mother that she still had a year to go) "One should keep a little weight on the face." Yes, her mother had been her usual unsubtle self.

"She was fine at Christmas when we saw her," Mrs. B said.

"Yes, I know but she's not well now and Michael sounds very

worried, otherwise he wouldn't have called me. He seldom does this unless it's really not good."

Mrs. B was not sure what she should say or offer to do. She felt affected by the news, but couldn't really say how. It wasn't compassion for her mother, but was there a touch of unhappiness and a daughter's guilt over duty neglected?

But Claire wasn't waiting for a response or offer of action from her niece.

"I may go up next week," she said.

"But you hate to travel even to Tobago," Mrs. B replied.

"Yes, I know I do, but Michael seems so lost."

"I can help if you need anything. We can help with the ticket. I can take you to the airport if you like." Mrs. B did not know what else to say. She couldn't bring herself to offer to go with her aunt.

"Don't worry, Lena. I just thought you should know and maybe give your father a call. I'll call you if I need anything, but please don't trouble Ruthie with this news. Ruthie has been through enough already."

"She has, Auntie, but I'll talk to Charles and see what he says we should do."

"Yes, talk to Charles and don't worry yourself too much. These moods come and go, and then she's fine again."

They said their goodbyes and promised to talk soon.

Mrs. B sat on the sofa in the living room. She had forgotten about Milly waiting for her in the kitchen. She was trying to recall the times she had seen her mother depressed. There was one night when she heard her mother crying in the living room with all the lights out in the house. She remembered going down the stairs; the whimpering sounded like an injured puppy. There was also the time in Tobago when her mother lay in bed for most of the week, leaving her father and the helper to prepare all the meals. Mrs. B spent most of the time with her cousins until the last day when her mother finally decided to get out of bed and join the rest of the family. Thinking now, Mrs. B realized that her mother must have suffered from these bouts of depression for most of her life. She felt worried, concerned but also angry. Simone had continually brought sadness into her life and she could not forgive her mother for this.

Claire also felt distressed after the call to her niece. She had not been able to say that Simone was very ill, and had been this ill before. It had been one of the reasons why Simone had to leave the young Mrs. B with Claire for those two years. Soon after Elena's birth, Simone had become extremely depressed and it was left to the housekeepers and babysitters to take care of the baby. And even though Simone had found a way to love the child, she would tell Claire there was always something missing, something she felt other mothers had that she lacked. In one of her darkest moments, Simone told Claire that she never wanted to be a mother and that it was wrong to assume that every woman wanted a child. Michael had wanted a child and in those days it was unnatural not to want to be a mother, even if some act of abandonment was to follow. The universe had played a dirty trick on them, Simone said. Claire who so desired children could not have one, while she, who never wanted a child, had been given a daughter.

*

In the weeks that followed their quarrel, Charles refused to take any calls from his brother unless they were about work and declined every invitation that Robby made to join him down-the-islands. Robby had attended the ridiculously lavish party hosted by Chow for the President and his men. After Robby had been pictured on the front page of the *Express* with Chow, the President and two of the most corrupt ministers, both rumoured to be involved in the drug trade, Charles refused to take any calls at all from Robby. Ruthie and his secretaries would have to handle it.

The day of the elections was approaching, the numbers at the rallies were growing and Chow was on the President's platform every night.

# CHAPTER SIX
## CRIMES

Two weeks passed without a single murder. It was an island record. This momentary reprieve, this small period of grace, was received like the host at Sunday Mass. No one wanted to ask how the peace had come about, or put goat mouth on the good luck. People just breathed a little easier, and lived their lives a little less cautiously, a little less fearfully, but no one was foolish enough to believe that it would last. Everyone knew that sooner rather than later, just around the corner, there would be another horror. After all it was election time.

Then it started again. In one weekend, ten people were killed; this was close to the island record of thirteen murders in three days. Of the ten killed, five were fishermen. Three of the fishermen were shot at two a.m. on Saturday morning outside a beach bar in Cedros. Three hours later, two more were shot thirteen times each in a fishing village in Blanchisseuse. There was an electrician and his girlfriend shot in their sleep, and worst of all a grandfather, grandmother and their grandson were chopped to death at six o'clock on Sunday evening after attending a relative's birthday party. This last crime was highlighted on the front page of all the daily papers, with pictures of the bloody bedroom where the massacre had taken place. Someone had even posted pictures of the semi-covered bodies on Facebook. The fishermen and electrician murders were relegated to page three.

Ruthie seldom read the dailies; local news came to her from television or the Internet. But the gruesome details of the murdered family haunted her because they came from the valley where she had grown up. She thought she recognized the grandfather's face in the photographs that the relatives had given to the papers. He was a thin Indian man with a side-part in his thick grey hair; he was standing behind the chair where his wife sat in a sari holding their grandson, who could not have been more than a year old at the time the photograph was taken. It must have been an old picture because the papers said that the murdered boy was three. The maternal grandparents had been bringing up the boy since his mother had died in a car crash just two months after the boy was born. The boy had lost an uncle in the accident as well. As she studied the photograph Ruthie was convinced that the grandfather was the old Indian man whose vegetable garden deep in the valley she and her father would pass on their walks with the dogs. The old man would always raise a thin brown hand to greet them. Ruthie's father would respond in the same way, and both seemed satisfied with the quiet exchange. Ruthie wanted to ask her father if he recognized the man, but he had withdrawn from her since she told him that she had found another job teaching history and English in a private high school. He seemed to take the news well in the office, but when he came home he said very little. The fact that he showed no anger, only disappointment, made Ruthie feel even worse.

*

That night Ruthie dreamt she was driving through the old valley. She passed the cocoa plantations. She saw the yellow pouis on the hills, the white egrets resting on the backs of the cattle. She saw the hawk that lived on highest branch of the African tulip, the small green parrots, the village football fields, the temple, the mosque, the church on the hill, and the bamboo swaying and bowing as though welcoming her back to her old home. But in the dream she never made it to her old house, even though it was where she wanted to go. She just kept driving through the same landscape until she began to feel trapped.

The next morning Ruthie got up feeling groggy. It was a bright, windy morning in San Pedro but her mind was still in the valley. If only she could go back to the time before her parents left the valley, before she met the Professor, before she lost Maria. Their lives had been jinxed after leaving that house. Perhaps their neighbour Mary had put a curse on the people who ran away, for never avenging her rape. Running away had not made life better; it just seemed to confirm that the other side was winning. The neighbours, rich and poor, should have declared war for Mary, brandished arms, shouted until their throats bled that no army of nasty, butchering bandits was going to make them run away from what was rightfully theirs. But they had run away and were still running into every San Pedro on the island. Before Ruthie left Boston she was full of compassion for the poor, but now that she was back home fear had taken over and the reality of constantly having to look over her shoulder replaced much of the sympathy she once had.

★

Mrs. B visited Aunt Claire the day before her aunt left for Fort Lauderdale, relieved that she had made no demands on her since she had given her the news about Simone. She would send her mother a get well card, even though she suspected that this was more suited to someone with a simpler illness, like the flu or even a broken leg. There were no cards in the shop that suited what her mother had. She made both Charles and Ruthie sign and wrote, "I hope you feel better soon." The moment she had written this, she wanted to scratch it out, and even thought about getting another card, but she sealed the envelope before her thoughts ran too far away from her. What should she write on the envelope? "Mummy" (but she seldom called her mother Mummy), or "Granny" – for Ruthie's sake – (she was sure her mother would hate that) or simply Simone? She opted for Simone.

Claire looked tense that morning and for the first time in years they did not sit on her small back porch but stayed in the living room. The curtains were drawn, making the room dark, even though it was a very bright morning. Mrs. B knew her aunt did not like travelling; going to see her sister was a great sacrifice.

"I spoke to Michael last night; he managed to get her to go for a drive, so that is some good news." But the look on Claire's face did not suggest "good news".

"I wish I were coming to help you."

"There's really nothing you can do to help me, Lena, and your father is there."

"I know how much you hate to travel. I really feel terrible about your having to do this and not me."

137

"You're starting to worry too much. In spite of everything Simone is still my sister and she needs my help as much as I need to help her now. You need to stay with Ruthie."

"Ruthie is fine now. She's found a teaching job…"

"Yes, I know. She told me."

Mrs. B had been irritated but not surprised when she found this out from Charles; discovering that Ruthie had taken the time to talk to her great aunt was more hurtful.

"Even with the job, she still needs you, don't you think?"

Mrs. B was uncomfortable with this idea but it seemed to be all that Claire could talk about. She offered to drive her aunt to the airport; she already had a lift, but accepted her niece's offer to pick her up on her return two weeks later. Mrs. B hugged her aunt, but as she drove away from Hibiscus Drive she was not sure why she felt so touchy.

★

That night, Mrs. B and Charles were supposed to meet with friends for dinner, but their plans changed when they heard the seven o'clock evening news. There was seldom any "Breaking News"; usually everyone knew what had happened before the TV talking heads confirmed the facts. But for once the news was new. Lawrence Blackburn and the Minister of Trade had been in a car accident. The details were still unclear but it seemed as though a ten-wheeler truck had broken a red light and slammed into the black Prado that held Chow, the Minister and a Colombian businesswoman, as well as the driver and bodyguards. The driver, Chow and the Colombian had been taken out of the car, from the "jaws of death"; the Minister, the bodyguard and the truck driver were not critical.

Within seconds of the broadcast Jackie rang. She had heard from a good source that the Colombian businesswoman was involved with human trafficking, that she had a brothel in Manzanilla, that the police, ministers, Chinese, Colombians, Jamaicans and even Chow was involved. But Mrs. B was barely listening; she was still trying to absorb the news.

After Jackie's call, she tried to follow a conversation that Charles was having on his cell phone; it sounded as though he was speaking to someone in Chow's family, either a brother or sister.

Then Charles stood and gathered his wallet and car keys. He halted by the door.

"Heading to the hospital. You not coming? Rachel will need the support."

"I'm sure she has all her family there already. That place is going to be a circus. They don't need more people around."

Charles couldn't understand his wife's response. She had known Rachel since high school and Chow was one of their closest friends, but he said nothing and left without her.

★

Mrs. B was alone at home. Ruthie was at her usual Tuesday night movie lime with Monique; she seldom came home before midnight. Mrs. B went into Ruthie's room and sat on the bed. The book on the bedside table was one she had seen Ruthie reading. Mrs. B liked the title *Truth and Beauty*. Parts of Ruthie's life were all over the room: her clothes, her jewellery on the dresser, her bags slung over the hooks behind the door, her books from university on the shelves, more books piled onto a small bench Ruthie must have bought recently, her laptop and note pads with numbers, names or phrases that seemed to be taken from books that she had read. There was a chequebook – Charles deposited money every month into Ruthie's account. Mrs. B didn't look inside it, but she did notice an ATM slip indicating a balance of $8,167.35. She thought about all the planning for Ruthie's arrival – the curtains, the bedspread, the painting, the shell soaps for the bathroom – all the effort she had made to make sure every detail was perfect. But now the room just seemed ugly – too many bright colours, too many goddamn shells. Ruthie must have hated it from when she first walked in, but had never said anything but thank you.

Ruthie got home before Charles that night. Mrs. B heard her unlock the door, go into the kitchen, then the bathroom. She thought she heard her on the phone, then everything went quiet again. Charles did not get home before three in the morning; Mrs. B had been falling in and out of sleep waiting for him to come in. He tried his best not to wake her, opening and closing the bathroom and bedroom doors very gently.

"How is he?" Her voice in the blackness of the room startled him; he thought his wife was asleep.

"Not good at all. A lot of bleeding, some internal damage, really not looking too good at all."

"And what about the others?"

"Rachel's holding up well, a lot of the family are there with her…"

"I didn't mean Rachel. I meant the other people in the accident."

"Well, the Colombian lady didn't make it; I think the Minister and the other two should be okay; they were lucky. The truck driver must have gotten no more than a scratch because he had to go to the police station to make a report."

While they were talking in the darkness, Mrs. B had a sudden desire to confess everything to her husband about herself and Larry. It would release her burden and stop her husband from feeling sorry for a friend who had done what no true friend should ever do. But she couldn't.

"Claire called to say that she had arrived safely and I spoke briefly to my father."

"How is Simone?"

"I don't think they're really telling me everything. In fact I'm sure they're not."

"Why? What else do you think they need to tell you?"

Before Mrs. B could think of a response, Charles's cell phone rang. He went downstairs to take the call. Mrs. B turned on the bedside lamp and followed him. Mrs. B was sure that it was bad news. Before she could ask, he told her.

"Hedidn'tmakeit." It sounded like one long word. Charles went on to say something about too much internal bleeding. He went outside without turning on the porch light. Mrs. B wanted to follow him but she didn't. He went on to make several calls into the early hours of the morning. Mrs. B did the opposite; she turned off her cell phone and took the landline off the hook. She went back into her bedroom, lay on her bed and waited for the room to go slowly from darkness to light.

She must have fallen asleep at some time in the morning because she heard Charles talking to Milly. Mrs. B felt as though she had been through a war. She looked in a mirror and her face looked old, drawn, with dark circles under her eyes. She dreaded going downstairs to face Charles. He needed her and she needed him; he had lost his best friend but she couldn't quite figure out what she had lost, or what she felt other than numb and angry.

Mrs. B recalled that Simone always said that when you felt your worst, look your best. She dressed in her tailored white jeans, a pair of pretty sandals, and an aquamarine blouse. She would not wear black; she was not in mourning. Ruthie was still asleep when she and Charles left the house. He was standing at the front door, car keys in hand, when he saw his wife emerge from the kitchen.

"You want to go together?"

Mrs. B hesitated before she replied: "I have an appointment at the hairdresser."

He just stared at her.

"I'll come over as soon as I'm finished."

"Right." Charles turned and walked out into the garage.

The morning was bright, there was a slight breeze and as Mrs. B headed towards the Savannah, the deep green of the northern mountains contrasted with the lighter green of the Savannah grass. Everything seemed perfect, especially the thick muscular branches of the sprawling samaans. The thought came to her that Larry would never see this Savannah morning.

The hair salon was abuzz with the news of Larry's death and the Colombian connection. It had been the main item on the radio and early morning television shows. As Mrs. B sat in the chair to face the unforgiving mirror, her hair stylist, after saying how nice Mrs. B looked, asked if she knew anyone in the accident.

"Yes, Larry is… was a good friend of Charles, the best man at our wedding. They went to high school together."

"He's not the one going up for elections?"

"Yes." Mrs. B said no more, though she could see that she had piqued her stylist's interest. They moved on to more innocuous topics, but two of the shampoo girls nearby were enjoying their speculations.

"I find the whole thing kind of strange," one said. "What a Minister and that other one, the fair-skin one, doing with an old hoe. Nah, something not sounding right there."

"Yeah, but that's the same one who had the hoe house by the beach. All them ministers used to go up there to get their stories

141

fix…" Mrs. B wished they would stop. She wouldn't put anything past Larry, but the idea of him sleeping with all of those "hoes" was not what she wanted to think about.

One of the girls came over and started washing Mrs. B's hair. "The water too hot?"

"No it's fine."

Mrs. B hoped that the girl would not bring up the Colombian story. It would make it hard to relax and enjoy a pleasure that she always looked forward to. But the owner of the salon had trained the shampoo girls well; they spoke to the clients only briefly and for the most part kept their opinions to themselves.

★

It had been a few months since Charles had actually been inside Chow's home, though it was only a few minutes from San Pedro. More often than not, Chow and Rachel entertained in one of their homes down-the-islands. Charles regretted for a moment the fact that he had refused Chow's last invitation to "party with the President", but he still could not imagine having to talk to a man who he thought had betrayed his country in so many ways.

Most of the people present were family members, but there were some managers from Chow's various businesses – in real estate, pharmaceuticals, and from his main office, and Charles immediately recognized two government ministers in their black suits with their fat necks flapping over their choking white collars. Their bodyguards stood nearby. Amongst this crowd of mainly French Creole, Syrian, and a few light brown business families from the north of the island, the ministers and their bodyguards stood out. Even though they had been a big part of Chow's life for the last few months, Charles could not help feeling these men did not belong.

From the verandah Charles could see Chow's and Rachel's daughters with a few of their friends. From afar the scene looked like a party, all these pretty young people sitting around a poolside table on a bright morning. One daughter looked exactly like Rachel with her long dirty-blond hair and slender body. For a second, Charles forgot both of their names even though he had been godfather to the elder. This was Chelsea, yes he remembered now, and the second was Sydney.

When Charles went back inside he saw Rachel's mother talking in the kitchen with his own mother. He kissed both ladies and they offered him coffee and a cinnamon roll. The two housekeepers were busy in the kitchen filling glasses of orange and grapefruit juice and placing cheeses puffs, meat pies and slices of banana bread on trays to be served to the guests.

"Where's Elena?" Naomi's tone was accusatory.

"She's on her way, she had a few things to do." Charles refused to give his mother more ammunition by telling her where his wife was.

Rachel's mother was usually a very quiet presence, but this morning she seemed unable to stop talking. She was worried about Rachel and the girls. She was worried about the business. She wanted Rachel to sell the house and move into a more secure place. "Like San Pedro, don't you think Charles, where you are. It's very secure, isn't it?" She didn't wait for a response. Naomi and Charles sat and listened to her until Rachel appeared in the kitchen and the room went quiet.

Rachel greeted Charles with a hug and a kiss on the cheek. Her face looked very thin, her voice was raspy and hoarse, but she looked calm. She had been saying prayers and rosaries with Father Murray and Sister Rosario, who she introduced to Charles. Naomi was embarrassed by her son's evident indifference to the introduction; she began to talk about how much she was doing for the parish – the fair, the clothes collection, the cake sale. Father Murray was one of the last Irish priests on the island, and Charles was reminded how as a young boy he'd always been afraid of the wrinkled white priests with their long chins, drooping flesh and scaly, spotted hands.

He learned from Naomi that Chow's parents were organizing the funeral with Chow's younger brother Paul. Then suddenly the quiet conversations in the kitchen were interrupted by one of the young men from the poolside barging in to say that there were newspaper and TV people at the gate.

"Auntie, we told Birdy to hold them by the gate, but they say that they just want to ask a few questions."

"Tell them we have nothing to say and ask Birdy to call Mr. John." Rachel seemed to have woken up from her trance. Birdy was the family gardener and handyman; Mr. John was the bodyguard assigned to Chow by the President.

"Do you want me to go outside and deal with those assholes?" Naomi flinched at Charles's uncouthness, but he didn't wait for an answer and went out to the gate.

The enemy comprised a diminutive man holding a mike, his cameraman and a young woman with a notepad. They claimed to be from TV3.

Charles kept repeating, "The family needs privacy now", and the interviewer kept asking if they had anything to say about the Colombian woman killed in the accident. Then a black Prado pulled up to the gate and Mr. John got out with another bodyguard, both six foot three, clean shaven, in black shirt-jacks, black pants, shining black shoes, and with steely stares. Mr. John confronted the TV crew, demanded their names and ordered them to leave immediately. There was a murmur of protest from the group but they soon got into their van and drove away. Mr. John assured Charles and Rachel that he would instruct the guards at the bottom of the hill to be more vigilant, especially for the next few days. Mr. John remained at the front of the residence for the rest of the day.

Charles had already left by the time Mrs. B arrived. She had taken her time. She knew the neighbourhood well with its neatly pruned olive trees, long driveways, and orange bougainvillaea hanging over the walls; Charles's mother lived nearby. The guard at the bottom of the hill waved her up as he raised the bar across the road. The news of Larry's death, and the Colombian's, had been on every news bulletin on the radio, but each time she heard his name it had startled her. She had no idea what she would say to Rachel or anyone else in the house. She saw the black Prados outside and knew there were ministers or government officials in the house.

After Mr. John opened the electric gate for Mrs. B, she walked up the long driveway to the verandah. Rachel's daughter, Chelsea, approached to kiss her, as though she were the one to be consoled.

"Hi, Auntie. Thank you for coming. Mummy is inside. I can take you in if you like."

"No sweetie, I can go in. How are you holding up?

"I'm fine, thanks, Auntie; everyone has been really good to us; we have a lot of support."

Mrs. B was surprised at the girl's composure. She reminded her more of Larry than of Rachel, though she looked more like her mother. As Mrs. B passed the other young people she could see the younger daughter, Sydney, who looked more distressed and was being hugged by a girlfriend. Mrs. B found Rachel, her mother-in-law, Jackie, Kathy and a Syrian lady whom she recognized but had never met, on the back porch drinking what looked like gin and tonics and white wine. There was plenty of food, drinks, jokes, and as little talk as possible about what had happened.

Rachel, though, looked ragged; she wasn't crying but her eyes looked tired and sore. Jackie and Kathy made room for Mrs. B, who didn't expect to find them both at the house so soon, but she knew that their husbands had made contributions to the President's party at Larry's request, which meant that they had now become part of the Blackburn's inner circle. This didn't really bother Mrs. B the way it had bothered Charles. What irritated Mrs. B was their new friendship with Rachel.

"Wow, you look great Lena. You got your hair done?"

This was not how she wanted to begin; Jackie's compliment made Mrs. B feel uncomfortable.

Mrs. B asked Rachel if there was anything she could do to help.

Rachel politely declined and told Mrs. B what she had already said many times that day about the funeral arrangements, how the funeral would probably take place on Monday morning since they had to wait for one of Larry's brothers to fly in from Houston. But little was said about Larry. Kathy restarted the conversation with the latest gossip about a mutual friend who had to sell his house in Fort Lauderdale because of his financial situation. They talked about how bad things were in the US, in Europe, and here at home. A list then followed of other families in trouble. Mrs. B took little interest in the conversation but she noted how happy Jackie seemed to be that she was now part of Rachel's group of friends. Jackie brought Rachel a cup of tea and a small plate of grapes, cheese and biscuits. Rachel kept getting up and going in and out of the kitchen. The phone calls kept coming. Then Rachel told Chelsea to put on the answering machine and she switched off her cell phone.

"It comes in waves," she said to Mrs. B. "I think I'm okay but then I suddenly feel as though I want it all to stop, to go back." Rachel wiped her eyes and Mrs. B held her hand. She had never held Rachel's hand before and it felt strange to do this now. Although Mrs. B didn't know what to say to Rachel, she knew exactly how she felt. The same thing had been happening to her all morning.

Mrs. B tried her best to spend at least two hours at the house, but by 4 pm she'd had enough and left when a new wave of family arrived. She promised to visit Rachel the next day and to see Kathy and Jackie soon. As Mrs. B walked through the living room she noticed Larry's wedding picture on one of the side tables. Charles, as best man was standing next to him. They were both laughing as though they had just heard the best of jokes.

When she arrived home, she found Ruthie sitting on the couch with her laptop by her side and a letter.

"I got in," she said without looking at her mother.

"Got in what?"

"A few months ago, when I was sending out my applications for a teaching job I also applied to a couple of universities to start my Masters in Lit."

"And you got in to one of them?"

"I got into two, Brown and NYU." Ruthie spoke without looking at her mother.

"And what are you going to do?" Mrs. B sat on the chair facing her daughter.

"I'm not sure what I want to do. I just started this new job, and I haven't even been home for a full year."

"It'll be a year soon," Mrs. B said flatly.

"So you think I should go?" Ruthie was upset with her mother's dry response.

"I think you should do what will make you happy."

"That's not what I asked."

"Isn't it?"

"Okay, Mummy, I'll make the decision myself. Thanks for the help." Ruthie got up from the sofa, leaving laptop and letter behind, and went into her bedroom, slamming the door behind her. Mrs. B stood up and walked out of the house.

PART THREE

# CHAPTER ONE
## HOUSEKEEPING

Above her head a fan kept making a buzzing sound, but there was another sound behind her she didn't recognize, a kind of garbled language. She didn't want to turn around, but eventually she did. An emaciated black woman in a loose-fitting, threadbare shift dress, with four plastic bags on her lap was sitting two pews behind herself and Charles. Mrs. B listened carefully to unravel the woman's words; she was muttering Hail Marys in between Our Fathers. No one asked the vagrant woman to leave, although those around her wished that she would disappear. There was an awful odour emanating from the woman or from something in her bags. The foul smell was beginning to spread through the air-conditioned church, overpowering the expensive colognes and perfumes that filled the pews. Charles hadn't even noticed the woman; he looked sad and tired. Ruthie was at the back of the church with Monique. Mrs. B could see almost every member of Rachel's and Larry's family bowing their heads or kneeling in unison. Rachel, Sydney and Chelsea would be first in line to receive holy communion from the Archbishop.

The thought came suddenly to Mrs. B that she belonged nowhere, but especially not here amongst this congregation. Charles had not attended Mass in decades and only for special occasions – a funeral, a wedding, or on rare occasions a baptism – but in honour of his friend he had decided that he would receive communion. With his mother in front of him, Charles joined the silent line. Mrs. B stayed sitting in the pew. She would not go, could not go. Not today. The devout, dutiful look on her husband's face angered her, and Naomi's self-righteous smile seemed to claim some kind of victory over her. Why had that woman always disliked her? Mrs. B could not think of anything she had done to Naomi – and she definitely didn't know about the affair with Larry. She suspected Naomi felt that she had taken Charles away from her, especially after his father died. Perhaps Naomi was jealous that she had gotten along so well with Charles's father, but everyone did. It was absurd that Naomi was still blaming her for the loss of both a husband and a son.

As the vagrant made her away out the pew, stepping over legs to join the communion line, she started to mumble something about Cuba and Fidel. Mrs. B saw Mr. John and another security guard appear and guide the vagrant out of the church. It was done so swiftly and expertly that only those in the pews close to the woman would have heard a slight protest. Mr. John returned after a short while and stood at the side door as still as a palace sentinel. During the service, there were those who wept neatly during the hymns sung by one of the best choirs on the island. There were others who cried more openly when Sydney and Chelsea stood on either side of their mother as the family followed the coffin in the procession away from the altar. But even the *Ave Maria* did not bring tears to Mrs. B's eyes.

After the service, Larry was taken to the family plot for burial. Charles went to the cemetery and later on to the house where close family and friends were invited. Mrs. B did not go to either the cemetery or the house; as far as she was concerned she had done her duty. Jackie and Kathy had asked whether she was going back to the house as though it were some event that Mrs. B shouldn't miss. This further irritated Mrs. B. She still couldn't get over their new friendship with Rachel, a woman they had torn apart so many times during their monthly lunches.

Ruthie went back to work; the posh private school was not far from the church and she had asked only for time off in the morning. She was making plans to leave in a couple of months, almost a year to the day of her return home. A few weeks ago when she told Monique about her plans to leave, it was the first time she had seen Monique look upset. Not the angry, swearing upset that Ruthie had witnessed on several occasions when Monique had fights with her "grandpa" (the name Ruthie had given to Monique's boyfriend); this was a quiet sadness.

"I wish I could leave too," Monique said. "I so want to get out of this place. It's just the same thing over and over again: same people, same faces, same limes, same shit."

"So why don't you go? Just leave."

"Go where and do what? I don't have all the qualifications you have. I wouldn't get in anywhere."

"You could get them, study, do your SATs and you'll find somewhere. I'll help you look; you could study design; you liked Art in high school, you were… are very good."

"I haven't done any painting in a long time. You know I just played the ass in school and I have nothing to show for it. I'm not like you, Ruthie, studying is not for me."

The conversation went around like this until they both realized that it and Monique were going nowhere. So they talked again about Ruthie's plans, but Monique, with uncharacteristic discretion, did not ask the question Mrs. B couldn't resist on the night after the funeral:

"Why are you going back? Is it for him?"

Ruthie was taken aback. Her mother was seldom so direct; her attacks were usually tangential, or tinged with sarcasm. The three of them were having dinner together, the first time in two weeks that they had managed to sit together and enjoy Milly's shepherd's pie. Charles had only just come home, having spent most of the day at Rachel's house. As he sat down to dinner she could smell the scotch on his breath.

"Going back for whom?" Ruthie tried hard to smile.

"You know what I'm talking about, Ruthie. This is not the time to play games with me. Not after everything *we've* been through."

"Yes, Mummy, *you* went through it. Not the rest of us, just *you*. Everything is always about *you*, what *you* are always going through."

Charles did not say a word. He got up from the table, put his plate in the sink and was about to head upstairs, but his wife refused to let him get away so easily.

"Don't you think we have a right to know, Charles? You may have forgotten everything, Ruthie, but we haven't."

Charles stood still and stared at his wife.

"No one asked you to forget." Ruthie's voice had lost its bravado, and now sounded shaky.

"You can't come back and cause all this confusion and then decide you want to go back to that sick, unhealthy relationship and do what? End up in the hospital again?"

"What confusion? All you care about is that I embarrassed you in front of your friends. You're probably happy I lost the baby." Ruthie was shouting now, tears streaming down her face.

And that was when Mrs. B called her daughter a bitch; a word that had lost its power in recent times, but not for Mrs. B and certainly not from a mother to daughter.

As the words flew out – "You selfish little bitch!" – she wanted to pull them back.

Ruthie left the dining room and Charles looked at his wife and shook his head. This was too much.

"You look at me all high and mighty but when we get another call saying she did some shit again, who has to go? I have to go, not you, me. I have to go and clean up all the crap, put everything back together, while you stay here hiding like a damn coward…"

"Right, that's it." Charles didn't wait for his wife to finish; he kept walking up the stairs and into the bedroom. Ruthie had already disappeared into her own room.

Mrs. B was left standing alone at the side of the dining room table. She didn't know where she should continue her rant, in which of the two bedrooms. In the end she opted for neither and for the first time since Larry's death she cried.

★

For days after the quarrel, the atmosphere in the house was tense; Mrs. B, Charles and Ruthie said very little to each other beyond what was essential. Only three days after Larry's death, Mrs. B had received more bad news. Claire called.

"We thought she was getting better. For a few days when I first arrived she seemed to perk up, but she's not getting out of it, and she won't take the pills. She won't do anything the doctors have told her to do." Mrs. B could tell from the pauses in Claire's voice that she was trying her best to compose herself as she spoke. Claire had planned to stay with her sister for ten days, but now it would be longer. Mrs. B agreed to take care of the house on Hibiscus Drive until her aunt came back, whenever that would be. A neighbour had been looking after the plants and turning on the lights in the evenings, but now that she would be away for longer, Claire did not want to impose on the neighbour's kindness. Mrs. B agreed to take over these duties. At the end of the call, when Claire asked Mrs. B if she wanted to speak to her father, Mrs. B said no; she did not know what to say, and the thought of hearing his voice made her feel anxious.

The next morning she got the keys for her aunty's house from Mr. Brown, a widower who lived next door. He had moved there a couple of years ago. He was a good-looking man, probably in his early seventies – tall, slim, though with a slight paunch, and with a full head of silver hair, which he parted to the side. His skin looked tanned, a little leathery. He spoke in a loud, booming manner, as though he had spent a lot of time in the military giving orders, but his words, although delivered in the tone of a general, were gentle.

"I hope your mother gets better soon," he said, but he could as well have said, "Hit the ground and do ten sit ups."

"Yes, we hope so as well." Mrs. B took the keys. Mr. Brown mentioned a few idiosyncrasies: the lock from the garage into the kitchen had to be jimmied slightly and the sliding doors in the living room were on the verge of becoming dislodged; she would need to open them with care. Mr. Brown also knew that "Claire likes to air out the study", so he usually left the windows open for a couple of hours every day. He gave this information at the gate in his plaid Bermuda shorts and navy-blue polo. Mrs. B would have guessed golf, but his racket gave him away and she soon learnt that his passion was tennis, that he went to the public courts almost every morning except for Sundays when he attended church (the same one as Aunt Claire). They agreed that she would water the plants, open the study windows but would leave the keys with Mr. Brown's housekeeper when she left. Mr. Brown said it would be no problem to put on the lights in the evening. Mrs. B said she could do this before she left, but it was clear that Mr. Brown liked the idea of helping her aunt and he seemed quite familiar with the house.

As Mr. Brown drove away in his spotless white station wagon, old but very well maintained, Mrs. B went to the kitchen to find a watering can for the indoor potted plants. But passing the door to the hallway, she turned and went down the narrow corridor that led to her aunt's study, or library as her aunt preferred to call it. Mrs. B could not remember the last time she had been in this room, but little had changed since she was a child. Then she had loved books almost as much as Ruthie, but never as much as Aunt Claire. The room had a musty smell; some of the books on the upper shelves looked dusty and worn. The newer paperbacks on the lower shelves looked less fragile. It seemed as though her aunt had been rearranging or planning to donate part of her collection for there were three piles of books in two cardboard boxes. One shelf to the left of the window was clear, but all the others were lined with what Mrs. B guessed were her aunt's favourite authors. Fat, thin, tattered or fresh, each book had its own scent, but a green woodsy smell prevailed. Near the window was Claire's old armchair; a burgundy and purple paisley-patterned shawl that Mrs. B thought she recognized had been thrown over one of its arms, but she didn't remember the tall modern-looking lamp next to the old mahogany side-table – which was bare except for a small glass vase. Mrs. B remembered it full of flowers, usually the yellow hibiscus from the garden.

Her aunt, who was usually quite easy-going, was only ever strict when it came to this room. As a little girl Mrs. B was not allowed to play any of her make-believe games in the library; when she did trespass she received a stern warning from her aunt: this was not a playroom but a reading room. Her aunt, though, had started a collection for her young niece on one of the lower shelves, and most bedtimes would read to her. A favourite book had been *The Secret Garden*, which Mrs. B remembered as the story of a little girl who had lost her parents but still managed to find happiness. At night, after a light supper, niece and aunt would both lie on the narrow single bed in Mrs. B's bedroom; her aunt would smell of lavender soap and there was the aroma of the hot cocoa she was allowed to sip as they took turns to read. The ritual was to say the *Our Father* before they began to read, since Mrs. B would often fall asleep during the reading.

When her parents took her back for good, she missed many things about the quiet times she had spent with her aunt. Even though Mrs. B didn't remember all of it, what had never left her was the bedtime ritual of milky sweet cocoa, her aunt's soft hands and the gentle voice that lulled her to sleep. She didn't need years of therapy to tell her that it was the loss of those nights that had created the distance and fed the anger that she still felt towards her parents. Even though her parents tried to imitate the scene in a big new room, (her aunt must have told them that it was something Elena enjoyed) neither Simone nor Michael could take her aunt's place; it was simply too late. She was about to enter the all-girls Catholic high school, and the teenage years were about to offer less innocent pleasures.

Mrs. B enjoyed the morning at her aunt's house; she watered the plants inside as well as those in the neat garden outside. The sound of Mr. Brown returning from his tennis at ten o'clock made her aware of her deliberate actions to prolong her caretaking efforts. Before she left, Mrs. B decided to borrow a book from her aunt's shelves; she noted a shelf that had a lot of books by Gabriel Garcia Marquez, an author she had tried to read a long time ago. She did not select either of the two old paperback copies of *A Hundred Years of Solitude*, or *No one Writes to the Colonel*, but took instead a hard cover edition of *Love in the Time of Cholera*. Her aunt had a paperback edition as well.

Mrs. B could not remember when she stopped loving books. As a child she was a voracious reader, even getting her parents in trouble with the family as a result of her precociousness. She read a little less through high school, though in sixth form she had studied English Literature. She remembered loving Shakespeare with a passion, but resisting Chaucer. Then came the year abroad, at Simone's insistence, since Mrs. B had no desire to further her studies beyond sixth form. Simone organized stays with family and friends in London, Paris, and a few months with an old family friend in Milan. By the end Simone felt that she had created a more sophisticated young lady, but Mrs. B could not confirm any change in her own self, except that she could now say that she had been to this museum or that city. As her visit to Martinique had come to prove, she had little talent for languages.

On her return from her year abroad she met and married Charles and Simone felt that all her efforts had come to naught. Charles was not a reader and Mrs. B herself began to read less.

Other wifely things took over and once she had Ruthie there seemed to be little time or need to indulge in a good book. Charles's family didn't collect works of art like Simone and Michael; they belonged to the local business class who did not give much value to these pursuits. They were not against them, they just simply didn't see the point. Although Mrs. B wanted to blame Charles for taking away her love of books, she knew that was her own fiction. It was not Charles's fault, in the same way that it was not Charles's fault that she had stopped doing many things that had once given her great pleasure.

For the next week Mrs. B found herself collecting the keys from Mr. Brown before he left for tennis. She would water the plants, and on some days she would even sweep and dust (something she very seldom did at home) and then she would settle herself into Claire's armchair prepared to read a few pages of her Marquez until she heard Mr. Brown's station wagon. The Marquez rarely held Mrs. B's interest for long. Indeed, none of the books in the study could sustain Mrs. B's attention for more than a few pages at a time, and this included her aunt's favourite, *Madame Bovary*, of which she had four copies. Nevertheless, Mrs. B enjoyed being in the study even if the reason why she was there was not a pleasant one. Her mother was sick and she should be cheerless and miserable, but in fact the time spent in Hibiscus Drive felt like a vacation from her life.

## CHAPTER TWO
## CONTAGION

Two weeks had passed since Aunt Claire had left for Miami and Mrs. B was preparing herself for the end of this timely escape. It was mid-morning when she left her aunt's house and drove to a spot on the highway where she usually bought flowers. When she lived in the valley she could walk out into the garden and cut the red and pink ginger lilies, the heliconias, or anthuriums, but now she paid ridiculous prices for what was once free.

As Mrs. B drove into their parking area in San Pedro, she noticed that Charles's car and Ruthie's rented car were already there. The sight of both of them sitting in the living room with solemn faces gave Mrs. B a hollow feeling.

Charles was forced once again to be the messenger of bad news. But what Mrs. B heard were not her husband's exact words; what she thought she heard her husband say was that her mother had succeeded this time around, that she was dead. In fact what Charles had actually said was that Simone *had tried* again. Despite all Claire's and Michael's best efforts, despite the psychiatrist's visits to the house, or the caregiver's efforts, she had still tried. Somehow she had managed to hide away a stash of the pills, and although both Michael and Claire thought she seemed brighter, they didn't realize it was because she had found some peace in the idea that it would soon be over. Mrs. B was listening now, her thoughts had caught up; she could follow Charles' words, and she too wanted it all to end, to be over.

They had decided to readmit Simone to the psychiatric ward where there would be round the clock surveillance. There was a pause before Charles spoke again. He was not sure whether his wife had registered a single word; she looked distracted, in some other place, not there with them. "This time she will have to stay for a while. Claire says they are too afraid to have her at home, even with the caregiver."

These were more words than Charles had said to her since the argument with Ruthie, who tried to console her mother.

"If you want to go up, you can Mummy, or I can go with you if you like. But if you want to go, we'll be fine."

"Why would I want to go up? Claire is there."

She left them both sitting on the sofa and went into the kitchen. Milly was at the sink, draining the pasta, preparing lunch. The radio was on Milly's religious station where the priest prayed for the entire day, in between testimonials of miracles that had taken place in the last hour or so. Mrs. B put the flowers in a large vase and told Milly she would arrange them later. She did not want to be with her husband or her daughter. She declined Charles's invitation to lunch as well as Ruthie's to see a film later that afternoon when she returned from work. Charles thought that she should call Claire and Mrs. B said she would, but she knew she wouldn't. There was a feeling of relief when they both went back to work, leaving her with Milly.

She had always wanted a sister, someone she could trust and talk to without hiding behind all the invisible veils she had worn to protect herself from what she was never quite sure. Although she had known Jackie and Kathy forever, she could not trust either enough to expose her vulnerabilities. If she let her guard down with her friends even a little, it was never for too long.

Only-child, lonely-child she used to say, though she knew that feeling sorry for herself at this stage of her life was pathetic. Even more pathetic was her inability to leave her childhood behind. Claire used to say that everyone had a cross to bear; that was just the way life was meant to be. She never liked to hear this. After Ruthie she simply didn't want any more children, even though she knew that Charles wanted another, wanted a boy. Her pregnancy was not difficult, the birth was not unbearable, but she did not want to go through the entire process again. She would concentrate her efforts on raising a beautiful, intelligent child who would not disappoint or be disappointed, who would not feel alone even though she would be an only child. For a while, she felt as though she was managing to hold her world in place; there would be no cracks for Ruthie like there had been for her. She had to ensure that Ruthie did not suffer her own fate; Ruthie would have two parents who would stay together and keep the marriage intact, no cracks. No crosses for Ruthie to bear. But Mrs. B had come to realize that the universe tested us until we failed, that it set up expectations to ensure a fall.

When her parents tried to put the family back together, it was her father who struggled to recapture some of what was lost, but their conversations were polite, perfunctory. Nothing that distressed her in her life was ever discussed. Now as an adult with older parents there was still so much that was missing. When her parents called once every fortnight they would ask the same questions and she would give the same replies. Everything was always fine; Ruthie and Charles were fine. And then there were comparisons about the weather in Florida versus the weather at home. When Ruthie lost the baby, it was Charles who gave them the news in his frank but edited manner. Neither Michael nor Simone asked to speak to their granddaughter; they sent her a card with a greeting about loss, which they both signed. The conversations after Ruthie's miscarriage would then include: "How is Ruthie doing these days?" and both she and Charles would say fine. Ruthie didn't seem to mind that they seldom asked to speak to her.

Mrs. B remembered that there had been moments in her sixth form years when she discussed the books, mainly Shakespeare, with her father. She remembered as a child, when her father was at the height of his architectural career, working with foreign firms on projects all over the world, how he would describe these places in detail to her. Mrs. B remembered trying to draw images of what he had related. She, too, had wanted to build cities. Her father was not a bad man, he could be generous and thoughtful, but he was weak, too weak for the likes of Simone.

★

During these personal trials in the Butcher family, the country had its elections. As the pundits had predicted, the President and his party were back in power before the votes were counted; they proclaimed a landslide victory. Although the opposition had put up a better fight than usual, only dreamers had any hope of change. The few fools who dared attack the President in public during the election campaign would now suffer for such disloyalty; they would lose their jobs, never see another promotion, or their businesses would be suddenly audited. Those who launched more barbed attacks, albeit on Facebook, would suffer more vicious reprisals.

The religious leaders preached peace; they never criticized the President but admonished their congregations for the island's sorry state; their sinful ways had brought the plagues of greed, envy, and divorce. Evil came in many forms: American, Jamaican, Lady Gaga and Dance Hall – and the Internet was a satanic force more powerful than alcohol and drugs. They told their congregations to be vigilant against the spreading virus of corruption. Corruption was contagious, and the path to salvation was to follow the path that Jesus/Allah/Brahma had made for us. Alleluia!

No one in the Butcher household voted. Charles had stopped voting a long time ago. Mrs. B had voted in the last election, hoping that a newly formed party would bring change, but their defeat was so absolute that she vowed to never again dip her finger in that damn red that took days to scrub away.

Her father had said long ago that politicians were all actors in the same play. They knew their roles, they knew their lines by heart and they knew all of their entrances and exits. Mrs. B's old aunts shook their heads whenever they spoke about "those" people – meaning the Indians and the Negroes, both the politicians and the voters – who did not know what was good for them since the British left; things would never change because *plus ça change plus c'est la même chose.* Larry had echoed similar sentiments at dinner parties: "Neither the Coolies nor the Blacks know what good for them, but at least the Coolies willing to work. When last you see a black man planting anything?" They had all laughed at their host's pronouncements.

At least Mrs. B would not have to see Larry on the platform smiling and pretending to be one of the President's men.

No one in the Butcher household stayed up to hear the election results. Only a few people were out on the streets celebrating, mostly paid supporters who drove around honking

horns and acting as though there was any real fight that war-
ranted a victory parade. Resignation, apathy, ennui gripped the
rest. On the days that followed, the country had to endure
triumphalist speeches in stadiums throughout the land, by the
victorious leader, with his shiny, freshly dyed blue-black hair,
his black suits and black shades which he seldom took off these
days even when indoors. Mrs. B had to endure Charles's rants
and raves when the leader appeared on TV – although this year
Charles seemed less vehement. He willed himself to feel angrier, but Chow's death had drained something essential from
his spirit. In contrast, Mrs. B felt released. It was not that she did
not feel she had lost a man who had been in her thoughts
throughout her marriage, and for whom, during the headiness
of the affair, she had even imagined leaving Charles. But she had
kept this secret from everyone, until the day, on the beach, when
she spoke to Yvonne.

Yvonne was talking about old lovers and she spoke of two
affairs with married men. One of the affairs had been with the
husband of a close friend, and Yvonne said that although she tried
to live her life with no regrets, she regretted this affair. "For the
betrayal, I lost both the lover and the friend, but the loss of the
friend was harder." The words she used were clear to Mrs. B: "*Un
abus de confiance*", "*une révélation*", "*une trahison*". *Trahison* made
Mrs. B think of treason, which seemed like an even worse crime.

Yvonne's confession let Mrs. B unburden the secret she had
been carrying for so long. It may have been too many cold beers,
or the freedom of anonymity, but Mrs. B told Yvonne, "I had an
affair as well, a long time ago. It was with a friend of my husband's;
he was his best man, his best friend and best man. They're still
friends and my husband does not know."

Yvonne looked at Mrs. B as if seeing her for the first time, as
if she had been transformed into something altogether more
interesting.

"Do you still see him?"

"We see him all the time. He's still my husband's best friend.
They belong to the same club."

"And you will never tell your husband?"

"Never," Mrs. B said, "it would hurt him too much."

161

"No you should never tell him. It is not worth it. *C'est vrai, tu as raison.*"

The truth was that Mrs. B had wanted to tell Charles at many different moments in their life – during terrible arguments about Ruthie or during their most intimate times together – but her fear and ignorance of how Charles might react, stopped her. None of this mattered any more: her Larry and Charles's Chow were dead, and there was no need to cause any more pain.

# CHAPTER THREE
## HONOUR THY FATHER AND MOTHER

One morning as Mrs. B was driving past the church where Larry's funeral had taken place, she saw the vagrant woman again. She was sitting on the church steps, her plastic bags at her bare feet. The brightly coloured floral print dress and the matching head-tie made it look as though someone had bathed and dressed her, but had not found any shoes to fit her size. Maybe there was a young daughter who took care of her whenever she reappeared at the daughter's house. Although the woman looked as old as seventy, she was perhaps her own age. Life could do that, add twenty years of pain to a face.

As she looked up to the clear blue sky, the vagrant woman seemed to be singing. Mrs. B pulled up to hear what it was; it sounded like a hymn but she didn't recognize it. A priest appeared at the front of the church, the parish priest, Father Mackenzie. As he walked closer to the woman, she remained sitting, but reached out to touch the bottom of his immaculate white robe. Mrs. B saw him pull away quickly to avoid getting it soiled. Then, as suddenly as he had appeared, he disappeared into the church.

Later, walking up and down the wide grocery aisles, Mrs. B kept thinking about the vagrant and Father Mackenzie. She wished she knew what song the woman was singing. She wished she hadn't seen Father turn his back on her. The hymn haunted her, maybe she would hear it again when next she attended a church service, though she was not sure when that would be. The grocery was almost empty except for a few housewives, some in matching gym attire (Mrs. B had enrolled at the gym several times, but never lasted beyond a couple of months). There was a woman shopping with her maid who pushed the cart and collected the items that her madame pointed to. At the checkout, the maid unpacked the cart and the madame paid with her credit card. The madame never touched a single item. Before she left the grocery with the boy carrying her bags, Mrs. B noticed two older women entering with younger women she guessed were their daughters. One pair was talking and laughing together, while the other pair barely spoke. Mrs. B tried to picture herself shopping with Simone but she couldn't imagine it. Yet the shopping she was doing was for her Aunt Claire, who was finally coming home after three weeks spent with Simone and Michael. The last time they spoke on the phone Claire told Mrs. B that Simone was still refusing to take the pills she'd been prescribed. Simone said they made her feel half-dead, like a zombie. The psychiatrist prescribed another combination of pills but Simone still refused. "Unless you watch her take them and then swallow, she finds a way to throw them away. Sometimes she even vomits." Claire sounded as though she was trying her best to stifle tears. "Michael insists that he can handle it, but I don't want to leave her. Imagine that, Lena, after everything, after all the bad things Simone has said to me, I realize that I still want to take care of her."

Mrs. B remembered how some days Simone would seem so full of joy, filling the house with her laughter so no one could be unhappy in her presence. It was as though her energy was contagious. But there were other days when she would scream over the slightest mistake that anyone made. After the raging there would usually be calm, a very still calm, and her mother would lie in bed and keep the master bedroom door closed for the rest of the day. Life with her mother could have soaring highs but the lows were unfathomable. And yet Mrs. B had never thought of her mother as ill, only selfish, unpredictable, unkindly critical, and at times unimaginably vicious. Mrs. B feared that Ruthie would end up like Simone, but as she left the grocery car park she kept telling herself that Ruthie was kind, not like Simone.

At the gate outside her aunt's house, Mrs. B felt sorry that she would no longer have the excuse of these mornings at Hibiscus Drive. Claire had given her the peace of an empty house that revived memories, not of her abandonment by her parents, but of the quiet times she had shared with her aunt. Mrs. B had also enjoyed her daily exchanges with Mr. Brown. She discovered that his name was David, that he had four children, two boys and two girls. They all lived in North America, two in Toronto and two in Texas. He was also a grandfather of five boys and one girl, who they all called Princess. Mr. Brown had gone out of his way for her, probably because she was Claire's niece, but Mrs. B suspected that a man like Mr. Brown would be willing to help any neighbour in need. Mrs. B even hoped that the relationship between her aunt and Mr. Brown was more than neighbourly. As she arrived, she spotted him about to open his gate, dressed for tennis. He recognized her car and waited for her to get out.

"I see you're not wasting the beautiful weather," she said.

"Yes, this is too spectacular a morning to stay inside and this breeze is fantastic."

"I'm not sure if I told you that my aunt is coming back tomorrow evening."

"Yes, yes I know. I mean you didn't tell me but I spoke to her on the phone yesterday." Mr. Brown seemed a little embarrassed by this and Mrs. B noticed the awkwardness.

"Oh, okay, we spoke to her as well." Mrs. B opened the trunk and Mr. Brown immediately rushed over to help with the grocery bags. "I just picked up a few things so she would have something in the morning."

"You are such a thoughtful niece. Your aunt is lucky to have someone like you. Not all families look out for each other the way your family does. You have your aunt taking care of her sister, you taking care of your aunt." Mr. Brown seemed loquacious this morning, excited, not like his usual steady manner.

"How is your mother doing?" he asked, resting the bags on the kitchen counter.

Mrs. B was not sure how much her Aunt Claire had told him about her mother's condition. Did he know about the suicide attempts or just the depression?

"She seems to be doing a little better," was all Mrs. B was willing to say. Mr. Brown must have sensed her reticence because he immediately began to discuss small details to do with Claire's return. He offered to collect her from the airport but Mrs. B said that they had already made arrangements to pick her up. Mrs. B wondered if he looked disappointed. Then he politely excused himself, saying that his tennis partner would be waiting.

"Getting to know you these past few weeks has been a pleasure. Your aunt always speaks so fondly of you and now I know why. I hope we see more of each other." Before he left, he cupped one of Mrs. B's hands in his own with a gentleness that surprised her.

The house was so quiet; the only sound came from the curtains rustling with the breeze. It felt like a New Year's breeze, though it was now April. After she put away the groceries, Mrs. B went into Claire's garden. She spotted two yellow hibiscus flowers in the hedge, picked them and put them in the small crystal vase on the side table in the study. Mrs. B sat and stared at the flowers and thought about Claire's homecoming and Ruthie's fast approaching departure. She noticed for the first time Claire's rosary on one of the lower shelves, next to *The Lonely Londoners* and *Wide Sargasso Sea*. The rosary used to be on Claire's bedside table, safe in her bedroom. When Mrs. B lived with her, they would say prayers every morning and every evening. She hoped the flowers would not wither and die before her aunt came home that night.

★

"It was difficult. She just wouldn't take the pills. Every day Michael and I would try to beg her to take them. It was a good day when she took them, a terrible one when she didn't."

Claire, Mrs. B and Charles were sitting around Claire's small dining-room table. They had just come from the airport. Charles and Mrs. B wanted to make sure that Claire was settled in, but as they were about to leave she invited them to stay a little longer. Her lean face looked drawn and tired; her eyes were puffy, as though she had gotten very little sleep in the past few weeks. She evidently wanted to talk.

"I have never prayed so much in my life. I prayed in the morning, before breakfast, before lunch, before I saw Simone while I was walking to the nursing home and in the chapel of the nursing home. I don't know how Michael managed to stay so calm, but you could see the tension and worry on his face. He could barely speak. He's lost a lot of weight."

Mrs. B took her aunt's hand and held it gently. She didn't know what to say to comfort her.

"Why wouldn't she take the pills?" Charles asked. This was so illogical. The pills made you better so you took them.

"She said they made her feel strange, she didn't feel like herself," Claire said.

"She's just not well and so it doesn't make sense to us, I mean her thought processes," Mrs. B said. She suspected that Charles wasn't just thinking about Simone but also about Ruthie. He was afraid that Ruthie would get sick like Simone; she had tried to harm herself once before, maybe she would try again.

Sensing this, she managed to say out loud what they had been unable to discuss for a long time. "Simone isn't Ruthie, Charles. I mean she, Simone, is suffering, she is ill, it's psychological. Ruthie's was more a cry for help, to create a drama to punish her Professor." Mrs. B could only hope that she was right.

Charles stared at his wife; Claire remained silent. She had always worried about Ruthie, but right now her thoughts could not go beyond her sister's illness. Besides it was true; Ruthie was not Simone, though she, too, was evidently capable of falling into darkness.

"Simone wasn't speaking much, but she told me one morning that it… no, that she felt as though she was in this hole, and something kept pulling her down even when she tried to get out."

"I am so sorry, Auntie. It must have been hard for you, I wish I had been there to help." Mrs. B felt very guilty. It was cowardly. There was a pause in the conversation and Claire yawned. It was almost midnight.

"We should go and let you rest. You must be exhausted." Charles was being considerate, but Mrs. B sensed that Claire didn't want to be left with all of these thoughts about her sister.

"I can spend the night if you like, just to give you a little company," Mrs. B said, looking at Charles and nodding her head, as though willing him to insist that she stay.

"No, I really couldn't ask you to stay. I'll be fine, I'm just a little tired, and, really, I'll be fine in the morning." But Claire's tone seemed to say the opposite, that she had been shaken, that she felt spent and fragile. Simone had always been the stronger one, or at least that was how it had appeared, but when Claire had seen her older sister curled up in bed for days on end, in a dark room, barely eating, barely talking, eyes vacant with no light behind them, it terrified her and almost broke her faith in life.

That night Mrs. B took care of her aunt. She brought her a cup of warm cocoa with a few pieces of lightly buttered toast, which was all Claire could stomach. Claire had a warm shower and then went to bed. Mrs. B borrowed one of her aunt's nightgowns before she showered in the guest bathroom. Smelling of her aunt's lavender soap, Mrs. B went into her old bedroom where she had slept as a child. It was the same single bed with the small white wicker side table. She closed her eyes but soon realized that sleep would not come easily that night, so she went into the library and selected a book by Edward Burton on *The History of the French West Indies*. It was old and dusty with a slightly cockled cover. Hopefully this book would put her to sleep.

Next morning Mrs. B awoke to the smell of coffee and frying bacon. It was just past seven. She didn't remember falling asleep and the book was still on the bed by her side, the lamp still on. Aunt Claire seemed less frail than the previous night, her face a little less drawn, but her quick, tight smile told Mrs. B that her aunt was still thinking about her sister. Claire had laid the small table on the side porch with her best breakfast dishes; she had covered it with a beautiful madras tablecloth with matching napkins, a gift from Mrs. B's trip to Martinique. Neither Mrs. B nor her aunt had much appetite for the bacon and scrambled eggs, or the buttered toast and imported marmalade, but both made valiant attempts to eat and chat, just a little, avoiding the subject of Simone. At one point, Mrs. B thought she saw Mr. Brown's head appear then quickly disappear behind the curtains next door, but she wasn't sure. Her aunt insisted that Mrs. B go back home after breakfast. She planned to go to church later that morning; there was a church bazaar that afternoon and she had promised to run the bookstall.

"You have to get back to Charles and Ruthie, I'll be fine. You always worry too much, Lena. You always have."

"And you never let me take care of you."

Her aunt simply shook her head and smiled. She couldn't reply because if she did she knew she would cry. She wanted to tell her niece that she had always taken care of her, like a good daughter. She regretted not saying this.

Before she left, Mrs. B made her aunt promise that she would have lunch with them at the house down-the-islands the following Sunday. Claire agreed, but knew that she would probably find a way of getting out of the invitation; she did not want to be amongst family, particularly Charles's family. It wasn't that they were unpleasant, but at times they lacked discretion, particularly Naomi, who would ask too many questions about Simone and she would be forced to find ways of avoiding the truth.

# CHAPTER FOUR
## DOWN-THE-ISLANDS

That morning, Mrs. B drove home in blazing sunshine; in recent years she had come to dislike the blinding weather of late April. Something about it demanded a kind of joyousness that she could not bring herself to feel any more; she couldn't remember when this had started. Charles, too, had once loved this time of year. It was the cricket season and almost every Sunday morning there would be a match against another side, or practice in the Savannah. He would be the one to call Chow early on Sunday to make sure that his friend was ready when he passed by to pick him up. Charles was a better batsman than bowler, but he was no Brian Lara. Chow, on the other hand, was a good all rounder and the team missed him whenever he couldn't make it to a match.

But since Chow's death, Charles had avoided the cricket club and had not been to any matches or practice. Sometimes during the week he would stop by the club and have a beer or two before heading home, but the last time he had played with the team was two weeks before the funeral. Much to Charles's surprise his brother Robby had been very considerate since Chow's death. He had called Charles almost every day since the funeral, and had offered to fill in for his brother at the cricket club, where he was also a member. It was Robby who thought that a Sunday down-the-islands on Monos would give Charles something to do, who realized that Sundays without Chow and cricket were difficult for his brother.

During his teenage years, and even as an adult, Robby had been a little jealous of the close relationship between Charles and Chow. They were more like brothers and he, Robby, always felt like the friend, an outsider who was happy to be included in any lime. As Chow became richer and more powerful, Robby's resentment grew, but like everyone else he was happy to be part of Chow's inner circle.

Charles agreed to join his brother and mother for lunch at the house down-the-islands. Robby and Debbie were planning a big family luncheon the following Sunday and they wanted to go down to make sure that everything was in order.

★

It was bright and windy when Charles met his brother on the jetty at exactly 11 o'clock. His wife had come home in a very sour mood and quickly rejected the invitation to accompany him. She was sure that his family would prefer it that way, especially his mother. Charles lacked the will or even the desire to challenge her.

Ever since Ruthie announced that she was going back to graduate school, his wife had been irritable, even irascible at times. It was as though she blamed him for Ruthie's departure and the fact that Ruthie had been awarded another scholarship. It was not something they had discussed, and he knew that their avoidance of the topic added to the heavy sadness they both felt about the approaching day. Ruthie had said that she would probably have to leave in late June or early July; she wanted to find an apartment and to settle in before the term began; she wanted to find a part-time job even though she had received a full scholarship. What was clear to both parents was that their daughter simply wanted to leave.

★

The strong winds made the sea choppy and the waves looked like chards of dark blue glass. Robby drove the boat with Debbie seated next to him; Charles and his mother sat behind them. The plan for the day was to give Blacks all the tasks to be performed for the lunch the following weekend and then they would picnic at either Turtle Bay or Chacachacare.

Any swim at Chac was always accompanied by a family story that Naomi related, and even though he knew it by heart, Charles had never gotten tired of hearing his mother tell the tale. It was about a great uncle who had been taken away from the family and sent to the leper colony as soon as they realized he was infected.

From the boat, the hills on the mainland looked as dark as the sea, though in some areas there were spots of light accentuating the many shades of green. As they went past the first Boca, they spotted a hill covered in bright yellow; the pouis were now in full bloom.

When they were younger, Charles's father would tell his sons stories about life down-the-islands. A family favourite was the one about Old Man Patos. On a moonlit night after one too many whiskies, their grandfather, Old Man Patos, at the time a young man of eighteen, decided to row from Monos to Gaspar Grande. It was a quest for love. The two young boys would always chuckle, no matter how many times their father told the story. He would lower his voice to a baritone before he said, "a quest for love". The young Patos was smitten with a fair English maiden whom he had met at a dinner party at a friend's house. He had received information that the English lass was to be found on Gaspar Grande. And so, after everyone had fallen asleep in the house, full of whisky and courage, Patos got into the boat and began to row and row and row. Patos went from island to island guided by the full moonlight, but he never managed to reach Gaspar Grande. He rowed past the Boca de Monos, he rowed past the island of Huevos, he rowed past the Boca de Huevos, he rowed past the Boca de Navios, and just before he was nearly swallowed up at the Boca Grande, Patos realized he was on Chacachacare, the old leper colony, very far away from Gaspar Grande and his fair maiden. "Aah, the things we do for love." Robby and Charles didn't care whether the story was fact or fiction – it was the way their father told the story, as if it was a very serious matter. Only later did the boys realize that their father was creating a map of down-the-islands in their young minds.

As they approached the jetty they could see Blacks waiting for them. No one could remember or even tried to call him by his new Muslim name but he didn't seem to mind. He tried his best to greet each one as they got close enough to hear him. "Morning, Mr. Butcher. Morning, Miss Debbie. Morning, Mrs. Butcher. Morning, Mr. Charles." Robby was an expert at docking the boat and he lined it up at the jetty with minimum effort. Charles knew he could not have done better. Blacks helped the ladies onto the jetty, and then Charles and Robbie handed up to him their mother's wicker picnic basket, the cooler and a cardboard box full of Pinesol, Lysol, Ajax, and Clorox, everything he would need to have the place "spic and span" – Naomi's phrase – for the lunch the following week.

Robby said little to Charles. He could tell that his brother preferred to be left to his own thoughts; he had come with them and that was all Robby wanted. When Debbie and Naomi came back out on to the large deck they had both changed into their swimsuits. Then Debbie and Robby walked with Blacks through the ground floor, then the first floor and finally up to the hilly grounds at the back. Even though they had not been to the house for three weeks there was little to tell Blacks to do except to prune the purple bougainvillea and bring the large pots of orange bougainvillea down from Debbie's and Robby's deck to the main deck where the lunch would be held. All the chairs in the storeroom, the beach toys – noodles, floats – should be cleaned, the tables wiped. They were expecting at least forty people. While the walkabout was taking place, Charles and Naomi sat at the long table on the covered porch outside the kitchen on the ground floor. Naomi had a gin and tonic while Charles had a cold beer.

★

When she found the lights off in the fridge, Mrs. B knew she had forgotten the announcement in the newspapers that there would be no electricity in the northwest of the island that Sunday from noon to four o'clock. No electricity meant no water because the tanks wouldn't work. The San Pedro Villas had its own generator, but there had been a problem with it all week and it still wasn't working. Although the day had started off bright and windy, by one o'clock it was very still and very hot. The fronds on the royal palms that had been swaying so elegantly were motionless. Mrs. B thought for a moment that she should have joined Charles and his family. At least she would have been able to have a swim.

★

They were passing the first Boca when Charles thought again about his wife and daughter. He remembered that when Ruthie was young he tried to tell her the story of Patos, hoping that he could pass onto her the knowledge he had been given by his father. But Ruthie didn't seem to find the story funny or even

173

particularly interesting. She enjoyed the water and being on the sea, but she would have equally enjoyed reading a book or flipping through the pages of a *National Geographic* searching for pictures of grasslands in Kenya or safaris in South Africa. Whenever Charles asked his young daughter where they would end up if they went through the Boca, she would always say, "Africa, of course", and Charles would tease her and say no, they would end up in China. They would choose different countries until they got tired of the game. As they played this game he would see his wife smile. She was so much happier then. They both were.

That morning, sitting at the table, looking out onto the bay, his mother had asked, "Where's Lena today?" She asked in a very casual manner, as if it really didn't matter, but Charles knew that when it came to his wife his mother's questions were never without a motive. His mother had already finished the first of what would be several gin and tonics; her burnt red lipstick stain was on the rim of the glass.

"She was very tired. Her aunt came in late last night and we had to go for her."

Charles did not bother to tell his mother about Lena sleeping at her aunt's, and he hadn't told his family too much about Simone's condition. His family did not really understand mental illness or the notion of depression. When things were not going well in the Butcher household, it was simply a matter of buckling down and finding a solution. If all else failed they could always go to see a priest at the seminary. They certainly didn't spend time mulling over and circling round situations as was the custom in Lena's family. Never once had Charles heard his father speak about being depressed; for him depression was a female condition, much like pregnancy.

Naomi didn't look at her son, just stared across the bay.

"I would love to go to Turtle Bay; it's been a long time since I was there. Your father used to love Scotland Bay but I always preferred Turtle Bay. You could actually see a lot of turtles there back then. Now I don't think you see that many."

"Scotland Bay gets very crowded now, especially on the weekend."

"Will she be able to come next weekend?"

"Who?"

"Lena. Aren't we talking about Lena?" Naomi seemed a little irritated.

"No, actually we were talking about Scotland Bay." Charles didn't know why, but he felt like goading his mother today.

"Okay, Charles," Naomi said, putting an end to his game.

"I'm going up to check on the water tanks. I'll be right back," he said.

★

Ruthie came home from brunch with Monique at a new Italian restaurant. She was surprised to find her mother napping on the porch on the daybed. Mrs. B had moved the bed under the shade of the overhanging branches of the neighbour's bougainvillea. As a little girl Ruthie had never liked to see her mother asleep; it made her think of death. She would wake her mother if ever she woke before her when they fell asleep together on Ruthie's bed during their afternoon naps. It had been a long time since she had experienced this anxious feeling, but she felt it today.

It was only a matter of weeks now before her flight back to Boston. Her father, unlike her mother, had come to accept the idea of her return and had even helped Ruthie with finding accommodation. They had visited several real estate sites on the Internet looking at possible apartments – very expensive ones on Beacon Hill, one or two in Brookline and more affordable ones in Kenmore Square and Cambridge. Her old friend Eddy, who was now at Brown, had gone down to look at some of the apartments to make sure that what they had seen in the photographs matched real life. She was hoping to get a place as far away from Cambridge as possible, since she had no desire to run into her Professor. Ruthie had recently learnt, through a Facebook friend, that he was now the Dean of his college and had bought an apartment close to Harvard Square, just a street away from the apartment of his good friend the Art History professor. The deanship didn't bother Ruthie, but his new house did, especially since she was hoping to get a place close to Harvard Square. So far she hadn't found anywhere, but there was still a little time, and she could stay with Eddy for the first month or so while she got organized.

It was only after she tried to adjust the temperature on the downstairs air-conditioning unit that Ruthie realized that there was no electricity, although she had found it strange that the security guards had opened the gate manually. The heat felt oppressive so she decided to change and go to the pool in the compound. On a Sunday there were seldom many people at the pool, especially on a sunny day like today. Many of the families would have gone to Maracas or down-the-islands like her father and uncle. Over the past month Ruthie had been swimming in the compound pool, even if it meant having to be neighbourly to people she did not particularly care for, but after an exhausting day teaching, the thought of driving to the hotel pool seemed too much. By the time she had changed and come back downstairs, her mother was in the kitchen filling a glass with crushed ice and grapefruit juice.

"I'm going to the pool, Mum."

"Fell asleep; it's just so ridiculously hot, and we still have no damn electricity."

Ruthie brushed a flower from her mother's rumpled hair. "When is Daddy coming back?"

"Why? Do you need something?"

Ruthie did not want to discuss her travel plans with her mother so she lied and said something about the car needing to be serviced. Mrs. B knew that this was not what Ruthie wanted to say. She could always tell (or at least she thought she could) when her daughter was lying to her, but she said nothing. Ruthie picked up *Half of a Yellow Sun* from the coffee table, went into the laundry room, grabbed a beach towel and left through the side door, mainly to avoid having to talk to her mother again.

★

The water at Turtle Bay was murky with a thick patch of reddish brown film on the surface. Charles and Robby thought it might have been oil from a tanker but they weren't sure. There were already four yachts in the bay, two of them anchored close enough to be tied together, allowing movement from one deck to another. One of the boats belonged to Debbie's cousin, Luke. They waved and exchanged greetings, and reminded Luke about lunch the next weekend.

When Robby drove off, Charles told him to go a little further into the bay to drop anchor; this took some precise manoeuvring because they had to be careful not to let the boat drift into shallow water. As soon as Robby was satisfied with their position, he took off his tee-shirt and dove into the water from the deck. He had always been the better swimmer of the two brothers, always the more athletic; in his early teens Robby had won several gold medals swimming for his club, "The Dolphins". From the age of thirteen to fifteen, he had even been on the national team, but at fifteen going on sixteen he started to rebel against the rigorous training, and once he met Debbie in high school, that was the end of his swimming career and his parents' dreams. Even now, after so many years, whenever she spoke of Robby's swimming career Naomi couldn't help but feel some acerbity, not towards Robby, but always to Debbie. Naomi had so many dreams for her younger son because she knew that Charles would never be a star. Charles loved his cricket, enjoyed the fishing competitions with his father but when it came to sports everyone turned to Robby; Charles was happy that he took the pressure off him.

Charles took a cold beer out of the cooler and marvelled at Robby's effortless crawl. He swam further and further away from the bay into the open water. When Robby got back into the boat Naomi asked if they could go to Chacachacare where the water might be clearer. Although Robby thought it was a little late to go to Chac, he wanted to please his mother and so after a beer and roast beef sandwiches, they headed out of Turtle Bay.

The wind had picked up again on the way to Chac. As they passed each Boca, the waves were bigger and Robby's boat, *J'ouvert*, left huge wakes that rocked the smaller boats behind them. Charles began to relax and feel lighter than he had felt in a long time. It could have been the beers, the sea, or being with his brother; he didn't care to think why, it was enough to enjoy it. As they entered the wide bay, they passed the dilapidated two-storey buildings. Each time they saw the rotten galvanized roofing that hung over the front of the building it looked on the verge of collapse. There were gaping holes where windows and doors should have been. There were vines and trees growing up around the decaying wooden structures.

For once, Naomi did not tell the story of the leper, or the Patos voyage, but reminisced about the picnics that they used to have on the beach with their father when the boys were younger. Charles recalled the camping trips when he was in the Scouts.

The water in Chac was light green and clear enough to see the sandy bottom. It had been a good idea to leave the muddy waters of Turtle Bay. They ate, they drank, they swam, they chatted about the upcoming lunch, the menu for the party, the boats to bring the guests, the caterer, and the bartenders. By five o'clock they were ready to head back to Monos before they returned to the mainland.

★

Mrs. B's day had been hot and frustrating. She was in no mood for company and had turned down a last minute invitation to join Kathy and Jackie at Maracas, and Ruthie's invitation to see a film with her and Monique. The electricity came back at five o'clock but Charles did not. He did not get home until seven that evening and the mere fact that he was in such a good mood added to Mrs. B's bad day.

## CHAPTER FIVE
## SUNDAY

Since his election victory the President had rolled out a "Stop the Crime" campaign. His first step was to fire the Commissioner of Police and hire a foreigner who promised to "stop the systematic corruption that had been allowed to exist in the police force". The newly appointed Police Commissioner, with his rough looks and even rougher cockney accent, spent ten minutes every night in the middle of the news broadcast, between the sports reports and the weather forecast, assuring viewers that kidnappings, rapes and murders had dropped since the day before. He had fancy looking charts to prove it. There was no mention of the gang wars at night, or the influx of deportees with murder records, or the three Chinese shot in their own restaurant at noon, or even a recent case of patricide when a sixteen year old girl had poisoned her father's curried goat. The girl claimed that since her mother's death, her father began to treat her like her mother. He beat her, made her sleep in his bed and demanded she get up early to cook for him and her younger brothers. The neighbours could not say whether they had heard or seen anything unusual between father and daughter. However, they would not go so far as to say he was a good father.

★

"We know it's a cliché but it's so true; where does the time go? One day you wake up and you're fifty but you still think that you're thirty-five." Mrs. B sipped her drink.

"How about those women who still think they're twenty-five?" Jackie added, followed by Kathy: "And they're pushing a good sixty."

"And then the kids, they grow up so fast and you can't seem to keep up; you want them to grow-up, but then they leave and what do you have left?" Mrs. B did not look at either Jackie or Kathy when she said this.

"What you have left is a life; you get your life back." Kathy smiled and Jackie agreed, although she did not look convinced.

The "girls", as Kathy liked to call them, were celebrating Mrs. B's forty-ninth birthday at Mrs. B's favourite restaurant. Mrs. B didn't like birthdays. She always felt that the expectation of a great day could never be fulfilled. Much like Christmas and New Year, birthdays were a set-up for disappointment. Charles was horrible at buying gifts, Ruthie usually forgot the day and Simone, her own mother, had never been one to celebrate getting closer to dying, as she would say. Aunt Claire was the only one who could make Mrs. B feel special on her birthday, but this year she had been so preoccupied with Simone's depression that even Claire forgot to call on the day. Still, Kathy and Jackie remembered and insisted that she have lunch with them. They all drank too many margaritas and mojitos and all too soon Kathy began to inform them about the many rumours she had heard about Chow.

"Apparently my man Chow was brushing with a few friends' wives – and to think we thought he only liked twenty-somethings and Colombians."

"You mean twenty-something Colombians," Jackie added and they all laughed, including Mrs. B, though the talk about friends' wives made her feel uncomfortable.

Kathy pretended to look upset when she told them of Rachel's shock when the lawyers dealing with Chow's estate discovered a secret credit card account that paid for expensive gifts that she had never received, or hotel rooms that she had never stayed in with her husband.

"Rachel is an idiot, always was and always will be, and Chow, as we all know is, sorry was, an ass hole." Mrs. B took another sip of her mojito and smiled as though she couldn't care less about what the two friends thought of her statement.

Both Rachel and Jackie looked a little surprised at their friend's vehemence, but they just laughed and agreed, even though they were planning to have dinner with "the idiot" later that evening.

★

The rest of the week went by faster than Mrs. B had hoped. Tuesday ran into Wednesday, Thursday became Friday and then it was the weekend. Saturday was slow at first. Then all too soon it was Sunday, the day of the party. The Butcher household was quiet but not at peace. Charles and his wife exchanged very few words. They both spoke to Ruthie, who was doing her best to disguise her excitement at the thought of leaving her parents and her home, though she still had brief moments of regret. She did not want to go to the party down-the-islands where she would have to face stares from family and friends, who were forever probing for whatever didn't seem right with her.

By this time, Ruthie knew that there were things her family would never ask. They would not ask what she felt about the miscarriage, the Professor or about what had happened in Boston. Once, when they were driving to his office, her father had asked in his roundabout way: "Are you feeling better now?" He kept his eyes fixed on the road. "Do you prefer it here? Is it better here than in Boston?" Ruthie replied that she was fine, everything was fine and that was it. No more talk of Boston. In order to explain it to her father or anyone else, Ruthie knew she had to understand it better herself. All she knew was that when the Professor told her, almost immediately after they had finished having sex, that they would have to stop seeing each other, at least for a while, because his wife was becoming suspicious, she thought her life was about to end right there and then. All the begging she did on her knees in that sordid motel room did not help. After she slapped him, pushed him, pulled his hair and tore his shirt, he grabbed wallet, keys, and jacket, then ran out of the room, calling her a crazy bitch. Alone in the room, his crazy bitch smashed two bedside lamps, yanked the wires for the phone, TV, and mini fridge out of the wall, tore down the shower curtains and knocked over the TV set. Luckily the motel had very few guests so no one heard the commotion. Everything seemed to have happened in slow motion, yet in her mind the actions were jumbled and fast. She couldn't remember exactly how every part of that night had unfolded. After her raging had subsided, she had in front of her the evidence of what looked like a war. She picked herself up from the dirty, stained carpet, put on more clothes (she still had on the tank top and underwear she had slept in), gathered her scattered belongings and left the room. Luckily the Professor had paid for the room in cash the night before. She could not remember how she got back to her university room.

When the affair resumed after she came out of the nursing home, the Professor would remind Ruthie about that night, how she had threatened to tell his wife, to take her life and to reveal all to the campus newspaper. Ruthie knew that the thought of taking her life had been there before her affair with the Professor. Leaving home had been harder than she had imagined. She hadn't thought it would have been so difficult to leave a place where she had felt trapped and stifled. But that first semester was one of the loneliest periods of her life. Even though the black students welcomed her to their island in the middle of the cafeteria, and the rich international students invited her to their weekly Sunday brunch at a fancy café on Newbury Street, she felt even more alone as the days passed. There were only two other Caribbean students she knew on the campus and they were in other departments. She remembered a story that appeared on the front page of the *Globe* about a boy from MIT who had drowned himself in the Charles. The eighteen year old Pakistani freshman had failed his end-of-year exams, would lose his scholarship and have to return home. His suicide note to his father and mother apologized for his failure. In the weeks that followed there were further articles about student suicides, about the incredible pressure that certain cultures put on academic success and the resulting shame of failure. But Ruthie didn't think it was just shame. She thought the boy had died from loneliness, homesickness. But it was more than that. The feeling of difference, of separateness had led her to imagine her body floating down the beautiful Charles River, or even at the mossy, stony edge of Mr. Thoreau's Walden Pond. There had been other times during her affair with the Professor, after they had had one of their weekly fights, that she fantasized about an overdose; the campus police would find her almost naked dead body strewn across the Persian rug in the Professor's office and he would be questioned, exposed and shamed.

After she lost Maria she could feel her parents staring at her again, watching her every move, waiting for her to try again. And there had been moments when she felt the darkness returning, pulling her down to a place that seemed too familiar. Those were days when she lay in her bed and could not move. All she could think about was Maria and the Professor. She could feel her parents trying their best to hide the fear in their eyes. But Ruthie did not give in; this time she fought harder. It wasn't difficult for her parents to convince her to see the family GP who recommended she see a psychiatrist. She saw the psychiatrist only twice. She took the antidepressants he recommended and they helped, numbing some of the pain. One Sunday she even attended Mass with her Aunt Claire. Then, slowly, she began to find a way to re-enter her life. It could have been the medication, the Mass or simply a desire to see those trees again in the mornings at the Savannah. Little by little the pain lessened. She didn't feel the paralysing grief but she didn't experience any joy either. There were no highs and no lows, just a levelling that seemed to keep it all on a flat, even plane.

After the motel fight with the Professor, Ruthie had walked around the campus in a daze. She did everything she was supposed to do. She went to class, went to work at the Art Gallery, but it was as though she was living in a different space, moving to another rhythm. When she spoke, her words seemed to echo, reverberate, make a loud noise in her head. She tried her best to avoid talking to others, especially her roommate.

The night Ruthie decided to take the pills was not a spur of the moment decision; she had been planning it for several days. She knew that her roommate would be out for the night (her roommate always slept at her boyfriend's apartment on Friday night and was never back home before lunch on Saturday). She knew that on this particular Friday night there was a party at Boston College and that almost everyone in her apartment building would be going. She knew that the concierge would retire to the back room behind the main desk by nine, after she made her rounds. Ruthie had made sure that everyone knew she did not want to go to the party. They wouldn't suspect anything in this; the others were well aware that this foreign student, although from a carnival island, unlike the partying Brazilians, kept to herself and would sometimes disappear for days.

Ruthie bought over-the-counter sleeping pills. She knew exactly which ones to buy, she knew the side effects, she knew how long it would take. All of the information was easy to find on the Internet; she read the articles online and visited a few sites on suicide, with links to sites of suicide poetry, or novels about suicide. In the previous semester Ruthie had written an essay on *The Bell Jar.* She loved the book but her Professor hated it and felt that too much had been made of it over the years. Her favourite part was the hanging fiasco, even though Ruthie had always known that hanging was not the way she wanted to go. That Friday night, she received an unexpected call from her mother. They normally spoke on a Sunday afternoon, but for some reason her mother wanted to speak to her that night. Ruthie was calm during their conversation even though her mother brought up the usual issues about returning home. Mrs. B always stressed how proud she was of her daughter, how Ruthie had surpassed her expectations, but Mrs. B had had enough of this studying business; she wanted Ruthie to come home as soon as she graduated, find a suitable husband, marry and begin a family. Charles and Mrs. B both feared that their daughter was becoming too American; too career-oriented, and although Mrs. B considered herself quite modern, there was no need for Ruthie to come back with too many qualifications, especially if she was going to be more qualified than a future husband. No husband wanted that.

Ruthie told her mother everything was fine and that she only had one essay left to complete, and that as soon as her exams ended she would come back. Mrs. B had gone over that conversation many times after she received the call the next day. There was nothing in Ruthie's voice that gave away what she was planning to do, except that their conversation was calmer than usual.

Before Ruthie opened the bottles she tidied her room, made her bed, put away her laundry, stuffed all of her dirty clothes in a garbage bag that she put at the foot of her bed. She didn't want to leave a mess behind. That was why she chose the bathroom, to make the clean-up easier, so when the reaction to the medication began – this was what she called it in her mind, medication – it would be easier for them to mop up a bathroom.

Ruthie filled her mind with these practical matters to avoid the thoughts that had plagued ever since she had started the relationship with the Professor. He said that she was the first student, his first affair, that the places they met for their hook-ups were all new to him, but they were lies all of them, piled one on top of the other, like a tall, stinking heap of shit, some lies new and soft, others solid and dry. She felt like a fool. Before the Professor she had been able to sniff out all the other liars with their sad, unimaginative lyrics, but the Professor had charmed her with his word magic. He was her first – she a virgin freak at twenty-one, saving it for Mr. Perfect and ending up with Mr. Prick.

★

It was Sunday, her uncle's down-the-islands party and her parents did not force her to come with them; perhaps they preferred to go without her. She could only think that she embarrassed them now. Her life had not gone according to their plans, especially her mother's plans. They did not take up her offer to drop them to the Yacht Club, even though parking on a Sunday was always very difficult; they only asked that if she decided to go out to let them know, or at least leave a note. This was an indirect rebuke for what had happened the weekend before when she went to a club with Monique after a late movie and had not returned home until the crack of dawn.

★

The drinking had already started; Charles had given Mrs. B a gin and tonic the moment she got into the boat. He held a scotch and soda. On the way down to Monos everyone was chatting, laughing, cracking silly jokes. The sky was blue, the water calm, the women perfectly made-up, gorgeously attired. All Mrs. B could think about as she sipped her drink was that two Sundays from now her daughter would be gone. They passed island homes – old, refurbished, brand new. They spoke of old families, the nouveau riche, the arrivistes. They all knew of a particular wedding that had taken place in Miami; who had flown up for that wedding; who would join the bride and groom for a second celebration in Tobago. Mrs. B nodded, chatted and laughed louder and harder after a second gin and tonic. A part of her would not be unhappy to see Ruthie leave.

It was a feast. Robbie had hired the best caterer, the best barmen, the best waitresses and the best DJ. He had the swagger of a man who knew that his guests could only admire what he had laid before them, not to mention the beautiful wife at his side, his two tall handsome sons (with their two gorgeous girlfriends also from good, old families). One of his sons was studying law, the other medicine. He pretended to complain – "Do we really need another lawyer, doctors maybe but lawyers?" – but was proud that none of them wanted to continue in the family business. In short, Robby had provided his guests with evidence of a life that screamed success. Naomi looked even prouder than Robby. She was moving from group to group, telling them to try this *hors d'oeuvre* or that dish. Charles looked at his brother and it occurred to him how much Robby reminded him of Chow. Perhaps Robby had always tried to be like Chow, but he had never noticed before today. By her third gin and tonic, Mrs. B was not letting Naomi get under her skin, nor any of Robby's self-satisfied friends. By her fourth gin and tonic she was feeling absolutely no pain – until she saw Kathy and Jackie arrive with Rachel. Mrs. B could have been eight years old, standing alone in the middle of her primary school courtyard while her best friends at the time walked away, telling her to go and find new friends. Fast forward and here she was again. Since Chow's death, Jackie and Kathy had grown ever closer to Rachel – the now even richer Rachel, thanks to the massive insurance she was in the process of procuring, the Rachel who in the beginning had played the part of the perfect grieving widow, but now seemed to have made a miraculous recovery. Instead of remaining mournfully homebound, she was a regular at the pubs on the Avenue, lunching at every new restaurant and liming in her down-the-islands home on Sundays. Mrs. B tried her best to smile as the three walked over and kissed her.

"Where have you been hiding?" Kathy asked.

"Same place. I haven't moved." Mrs. B smiled even wider.

"We tried to call about coming with us today but we couldn't get you." Jackie looked a little embarrassed.

"Really, when did you call?"

Jackie said she wasn't sure. Then they told Mrs. B that they were heading for the bar, since the roving barmen were taking too long to find them. As they walked away from her Mrs. B kept berating herself for the silly primary school pain she was feeling, but she knew that, child or adult, rejection and betrayal felt the same.

By midnight, the whole party of sixty guests and twelve staff were drunk. Many would not remember the crossing, and many would forget how choppy the waves were because of the wind, or that fact that it drizzled after they passed the second Boca, or that two married couples had made plans to try swinging the following night, or that Rachel cried in the dark while everyone else on her boat was singing along to Cyndi Lauper hits from the eighties, including Charles and Mrs. B.

# CHAPTER SIX
## DEPARTURES – TRINIDAD JULY 2010

They left the house in sun, with light rain falling like fine grains of salt. As they drove past the entrance to San Pedro, Ruthie said her last goodbyes to the guards, the one they called Ping and to Mr. Richard. At the intersection, the boys were still trying to wipe the windshields of the Audis, the Range Rovers and Benzes for a dollar. From the highway the sea looked as flat as a dark satin sheet.

Ruthie broke the silence. "Can we go around the Savannah instead of heading straight up the highway?"

It would take slightly longer, but her father agreed. He could feel his wife's disapproval but he didn't care. He wanted to please Ruthie, to give her whatever she wanted.

At the Savannah, with the midmorning sun, light rain, shimmering green leaves and grass, Ruthie realized that this was what she would miss when she thought of home: not the valley, not the sea, not the lush vegetation, not the hills, not the flowering bougainvillea along the walls in San Pedro, but the Savannah. No one spoke as they drove around what they called the biggest roundabout in the world, and then they headed up the hill passing the hotel where Ruthie had spent so many days at the poolside. She remembered swimming in the pool when she was very pregnant with Maria. The water made her feel so light and when she floated she would laugh at her bulging stomach bursting out of the water like a volcano. The last Sunday before she left, without telling her parents, she had gone to church with Great Aunt Claire, who was happy to finally spend some time with this niece she barely knew. Ruthie, who had spent very little time in church since she left for university, had decided that she wanted to say a prayer for Maria before leaving the island; it felt like a way of making peace. Aunt Claire had arranged with Father Alleyne, the parish priest, to pray with them at the church followed by lunch at Hibiscus Drive. Ruthie was quiet during the Mass; she remembered very little from her Roman Catholic high school days, but the sounds and rhythms of the words began to come back to her. After the private Mass, Father Alleyne talked to her about loss and the pain of grieving; Ruthie was happy that the rest of the lunch was not taken up by sermons and parables. Father Alleyne and Mr. Brown, who had also been invited to lunch, spoke mostly about sorry state of West Indies cricket and who would win Wimbledon that year.

★

Back on the highway there were fewer cars on the road than Charles had expected; school was out and the traffic flowed until they got to the turn off by one of the Malls in the East. Charles questioned Ruthie about how she was going to get from Logan Airport to Harvard Square. Mrs. B said nothing, never took off her shades and stared out of the window for most of the drive, only cautioning her husband once or twice about his speed on the slippery road.

Charles dropped them off at the departure terminal. The porter took the two bags, the two women stepped out and Charles drove away to park the car. The airport was bustling, busy with vacationers, some coming in but most getting off the island. Ruthie and her mother could find nothing to say to each other; it was not just this particular morning, but ever since Ruthie had said that she wanted to go back to Boston. Both felt uncomfortable without Charles to form a bridge between them. To break the silence, Mrs. B asked Ruthie if she wanted newspapers for the plane, or chewing gum for her ears, or a Jamaican pattie, or a caffè latte. Ruthie declined every offer, though she knew that her mother was simply looking for an excuse to do something, anything besides stand in line with her.

"I wouldn't mind some doubles. I think I saw a vendor in front of the Tobago Arrivals."

"Pepper or not?"

"Just slight pepper please."

189

She watched her mother walk away with her neat, short steps; she wore a wrap dress, with a green and white floral print. She had recently trimmed and coloured her hair a darker brown, and the bob suited her mother's slim face and fine features. Her mother had always protected her light-brown skin from the sun, telling Ruthie that she should avoid getting too dark because of UV rays, skin cancer etcetera. Ruthie never believed that this was the real reason. She had always felt that her mother just did not want a daughter who was too dark, especially since Charles's family were so fair skinned, but they had never really discussed this – like so many other things. Ruthie had tried very hard but she knew, now more than ever, that she would never live up to her mother's expectations. Perhaps no one could. Had her mother been more like her father, life might have been different. He had never placed this pressure of success on her. He hadn't given her the heavy burden of perfection, maybe because he, unlike her ambitious Uncle Robby, did not place any real expectations on himself. Her father seemed content to have a quiet, simple life, to keep his father's business alive and well, to take care of his wife and daughter, to spend time with the friends he had known since primary school, and when he had the hours to spare away from the cricket field, to be on the sea, in his boat down-the-islands, just like Grandpa Gerry.

"I'll miss you so much, baby."

"I'll miss you too."

The couple in front of Ruthie were hugging, groping and pecking each other on the cheeks and lips. He was local, tall, brown, shaven head, perfectly shaped goatee, broad shoulders, slim waist, a swimmer's body, in a white tee and dark jeans. He was hugging a blond girl, a little heavy on the hips, very busty and wearing a tightfitting baby-tee to exaggerate her assets. Ruthie couldn't help but look at the beautiful specimen of a man in front of her; she envied the blond girl, wished his hands were on her hips, wished he was whispering something rude in her ears, and the girl was the one looking on with envy.

Suddenly she felt someone grab her by the waist. The couple turned around when they heard Ruthie let out a shriek.

"Surprise, *chica*!" Monique held her waist.

"What the hell are you doing here?"

"I came to see you off, idiot; I didn't want to say anything last night."

"Sure, you don't even remember last night!"

Monique laughed and hugged Ruthie again. It made Ruthie feel good.

The previous night Ruthie, Monique and Monique's latest beau, "Bajan" Barry, were on the Avenue, bar hopping. Monique had gotten a driver from her father's business to shuttle them around, giving them permission to drink as much tequila and vodka as they liked. Ruthie didn't have that much to drink – she hated to fly with a hangover – and had looked on as Monique and Barry got completely plastered. Ruthie did not get home until four am that morning, too pub-happy to realize that her mother was still awake. Mrs. B had awoken at two am and was unable to fall asleep again after she checked and saw that Ruthie was not in her room. Ruthie had spent the earlier part of the evening with her parents, dining at a new Japanese restaurant. Charles chose the spot because he knew how much Ruthie liked sushi, even though he would have preferred Chinese. The restaurant's modern, minimalist interior impressed his wife who felt that the island was at least becoming more sophisticated. Ruthie agreed and said that without the crime and the corruption they had an amazing culture. Mrs. B laughed sarcastically and said, "Yes we have an amazing culture of crime, corruption and carnival. How lovely." As soon as she had said this, she realised how much she sounded like her mother, Simone. Charles looked serious; he wanted to say to his daughter: Why leave if you love it so much? Stay here with your mother and me; things will get better; the house will be calmer; you can be happy here. Charles wanted to say this and so much more, but the words would not come.

Ruthie and Monique were still chatting when Charles and Mrs. B returned. Ruthie was almost at the counter. Mrs. B was holding a brown paper bag with Ruthie's doubles, Charles had the newspapers under his arm. Monique embraced both parents and said she had to go to the washroom.

"I didn't know she was coming." Mrs. B handed the doubles

over to Ruthie, who put the greasy brown paper bag into her handbag.

"Neither did I. Monique is just so sweet."

"I thought it was just going to be us, just family."

Charles could see that his wife was irritated that Monique had invaded the family space, guessing that she didn't want a witness to the obvious discomfort she felt at her daughter's departure. He too would have preferred to have his daughter a moment longer before Monique drew all her attention.

Monique did not stay much longer after her return from the bathroom. She excused herself, saying that she was sure they wanted to spend some time alone as a family. Although they insisted that it was not a problem, Monique gave her friend one last tight hug: "Bye, Uncle, Auntie and see you soon, *chica*." Ruthie didn't cry easily but she felt the tears coming as Monique walked away. Now she wanted to cut short the possibility of a prolonged airport wait with her parents. She wanted to leave them and go through security before she completely lost her composure.

"So we'll talk about Christmas," Charles said as he hugged his daughter for the last time.

"Yes, we will, if not Christmas then definitely Easter," Ruthie said, moving towards her mother.

"You have a safe flight and call us when you get in." Mrs. B hugged Ruthie tighter than she had expected to and then let her go.

"I love you both," Ruthie said, before she walked through the revolving doors, only looking back once before she showed the guard her documents, not turning back for a last wave that her father was ready to give.

They did not wait around to make sure that the flight left on time. When Ruthie had first gone away to university they would wait until the flight took off, just to make sure she was okay. Once or twice there had been eight-hour delays and even a cancellation.

Outside, the rain had stopped and the day was suddenly very hot and filled with a blinding light. Charles and Mrs. B walked quietly to the car. As they approached Port of Spain Charles asked his wife if she wanted to get something to eat; her first instinct was to say no, but then she changed her mind. "Yes," she said. He seemed to have been expecting her usual no, so he paused for a moment and suggested the same sushi restaurant she had liked, where they had eaten with Ruthie.

"No," she said, "Why don't we have Chinese?"

And Charles smiled because he knew she didn't really like Chinese, but all the same he was ready to accept this gesture of kindness.

**THE END**

# ABOUT THE AUTHOR

Elizabeth Walcott-Hackshaw is a Senior Lecturer in French and Francophone Literatures in the Department of Modern Languages and Linguistics, The University of the West Indies, St Augustine, Trinidad and Tobago. Her publications include *Border Crossings: A Trilingual Anthology of Caribbean Women Writers* (2012), co-edited with Nicole Roberts, *Echoes of the Haitian Revolution 1804-2004* (2008) and *Reinterpreting the Haitian Revolution and its Cultural Aftershocks (1804-2004)* (2006) co-edited with Martin Munro. *Four Taxis Facing North*, her first collection of short stories, was published in 2007. *Four Taxis Facing North* was translated into Italian in 2010 by Giuseppe Sofo.

She writes:

"I left Trinidad at eighteen years old to study at Boston University where I received a BA degree in French and English, followed by a Masters and PhD in French. While at Boston University I took several Creative Writing courses with Leslie Epstein, Rosanna Penn Warren and Sue Millar. They were all very supportive and encouraging. My first short story was published in 1987 while I was studying in Boston. My Creative Writing Professor Raymond Kennedy encouraged me to publish the short story, "The Boulevard", in the Italian journal Spazio Umano. I left Boston in 1992 to return to Trinidad. It was, to put it mildly, an eventful year in my life I got married to my husband David and my father won the Nobel Prize for Literature. I have two teenage children my son Dylan is eighteen and my daughter Amy is fifteen. I started to teach French and Franco-Caribbean Literature at the University of the West Indies in 1999. I am presently the Deputy Dean of Graduate Studies and Research in the Faculty of Humanities and Education and I continue to lecture on French Caribbean Literature and the French novel in the 19th. century. The beautiful Santa Cruz Valley is still my home."

Raymond Ramcharitar
*The Island Quintet: Five Stories*
ISBN: 9781845230753; pp. 232; pub. 2009; £8.99

Raymond Ramcharitar's Trinidad is a globalised island with permeable borders, frequent birds of passage, and outposts in New York and London. One of the collection's outstanding qualities is that it is both utterly contemporary and written with a profound and disturbed sense of the history that shapes the island. As befits fiction from the home of carnival and mas', it is a collection much concerned with the flesh – often in transgressive forms as if characters are driven to test their boundaries – and with the capacity of its characters to reinvent themselves in manifold, and sometimes outrageous disguises. One of the masks is race, and the stories are acerbically honest about the way tribal loyalties distort human relations. Its tone ranges from the lyric – Trinidad as an island of arresting beauty – to a seaminess of the most grungy kind. In the novella, 'Froude's Arrow', Ramcharitar has written a profound fiction that tells us where the Caribbean currently is in juxtaposing the deep, still to be answered questions about island existence (the fragmentations wrought by history, the challenges of smallness in the global market, race and class divides) and the scrabbling for survival, fame and fortune that arouse the ire of Ramcharitar's acerbic and satirical vision.

Barbara Jenkins
*Sic Transit Wagon*
ISBN: 9781845232146; pp. 180; pub. 2013; £8.99

"Barbara Jenkins writes with wit, wisdom and a glorious sense of place. In stories that chart a woman's life, and that of her island home, this triumphant debut affirms a lifetime of perceptive observation of Caribbean life and society."

Ellah Allfrey, *Granta Magazine*

The stories in *Sic Transit Wagon* move from the all-seeing naivete of a child narrator trying to make sense of the world of adults, through the consciousness of the child-become mother, to the mature perceptions of the older woman taking stock of her life. Set over a time-span from colonial era Trinidad to the hazards and alarms of its postcolonial present, at the core of these stories is the experience of uncomfortable change, but seen with a developing sense of its constancy as part of life, and the need for acceptance.

Keith Jardim
*Near Open Water*
ISBN: 9781845231880; pp. 168; pub. 2011;  £8.99

These stories present, in writing that is both meticulous and poetic, a Caribbean world of unparalleled natural beauty, and societies that seethe on the edge of chaos, where crime encompasses both the rulers and the ruled, and where representatives of the state are as out of control as the youth Cynthia witnesses hacking off the hand of an old woman in a casual robbery. We enter this world through the perceptions of both those struggling for survival at the base of society and members of the old elites facing the consequences of past privilege in the reality of present insecurity. The stories stare hard into the abyss, at times taking us to hallucinatory places where nothing is certain. What is certain is the energy and precision in the stories' subtle edge of moral rigour in exploring the inner lives of those who fail to see that their "minor" deceits and evasions contribute to the "fire in the city". In such sympathetically drawn characters as Nello, the former car-thief now trying to do the right thing, or the memorably eccentric Dr Edric Traboulay with his intimate relationship to the natural world, we are offered glimpses of possibility. This is fiction that calls a society to see itself clearly, though about the revelatory power of writing the author is modestly ambivalent, as the powerful title story so shockingly reveals.